Gwyneth Rees is half Welsh and half English and grew up in Scotland. She went to Glasgow University and qualified as a doctor in 1990. She is a child and adolescent psychiatrist but has now stopped practising so that she can write full-time. She is the author of *Mermaid Magic*, *Fairy Dust*, *Fairy Treasure*, *Fairy Dreams*, *Cosmo and the Magic Sneeze*, *Cosmo and the Great Witch Escape* and, for older readers, *The Mum Hunt*, *The Mum Detective*, *My Mum's from Planet Pluto* and *The Making of May*. She lives in London with her two cats.

Visit www.gwynethrees.com

fairy gold

A naughty fairy causes trouble

Gwyneth Rees

Illustrated by Emily Bannister

MACMILLAN CHILDREN'S BOOKS

First published 2006 by Macmillan Children's Books
a division of Macmillan Publishers Limited
20 New Wharf Road, London N1 9RR
Basingstoke and Oxford
www.panmacmillan.com

Associated companies throughout the world

ISBN 978-0-330-43938-1

5 7 9 8 6

A CIP catalogue record for this book is available from
the British Library.

Printed and bound in Great Britain by Mackays of Chatham plc, Kent

To my sister, Anna,
with love

1

Lucy lay in bed, listening to her parents saying goodnight to her little sister, Isobel, in the next room. 'Leave your tooth where the fairies can find it easily, Izzy,' her mother said.

'I'll leave it under my pillow,' Izzy replied, sounding excited. Izzy was six and she believed in fairies, whereas Lucy, who was two years older, thought that believing in fairies was just silly.

'Not too far under your pillow,' Dad told Izzy. 'You don't want the poor tooth fairy to

get squashed under there when she goes looking for it.'

Izzy giggled.

Lucy rolled her eyes. She didn't believe in the tooth fairy and as a consequence she had all her baby teeth saved in a little pouch inside her jewellery box.

The reason Lucy didn't believe in fairies was that her half-brother, Thomas, who was eleven, had proved to her when she was Izzy's age that it was your mum and dad who exchanged your teeth for coins when you left them under your pillow. Lucy and Izzy had the same dad as Thomas, but a different mum. Their dad had been married twice, first to Thomas's mum and then to Lucy and Izzy's. Thomas and his mother lived several hours' drive away from them and Thomas only came to stay in the school holidays. He had told Lucy once

2

that he didn't think it was fair that he hadn't lived in the same house as his dad since he was a baby, whereas Lucy and Izzy had lived with him all their lives. Lucy had felt sorry for Thomas when he said that, because she knew she'd probably feel the same if she was the one whose mum and dad had got divorced. But Thomas could behave pretty badly sometimes when he came to stay with them, and Lucy always felt a lot less sorry for him then.

Thomas had been staying with them the night Lucy had lost her first tooth two years earlier, and when she had put it under her pillow for the tooth fairy, Thomas had told her she was being stupid. He had deliberately stayed awake after Lucy went to sleep and had shouted out when he'd heard Lucy's mum creep into Lucy's bedroom. Lucy had woken up just as her mum was putting her hand under Lucy's pillow, and Lucy had stopped believing in fairies from that moment on, even though her mum had said she was only checking to see if the tooth fairy had been yet. Lucy's mum and dad had both been really cross with Thomas about that, she remembered now.

Izzy, however, still believed passionately in fairies, despite Thomas also telling *her* that the tooth fairy wasn't real. Izzy said she didn't believe Thomas because she had seen fairies on more than one occasion, with her own eyes. Thomas reckoned that Izzy couldn't tell the difference between make-believe and reality and he was always teasing her about it, especially when Izzy put on her fairy outfit and pretended to be a fairy queen, which Thomas thought was very funny. Lucy was more of a tomboy

than Izzy and she hated wearing girly clothes, so she tended to get on better with Thomas than Izzy did – though it was difficult to get on with Thomas for the whole time he was there, because sooner or later he always got into a bad temper about something.

Tonight, after they had closed Izzy's door, Lucy's parents came into her bedroom. 'I know you don't think the tooth fairy is real, darling, but don't go spoiling it for Izzy the way Thomas spoilt it for you, will you?' her mother whispered as she leaned over to give Lucy a kiss goodnight.

'Don't worry. I won't tell her it's just you and Dad who take her tooth away and leave her the money, if that's what you mean,' Lucy whispered back.

'How could you even think such a

thing?' her dad protested, reaching out to tickle her.

'Because it's true!' Lucy retorted. But her mother was holding her finger over her lips to tell her to shush now, as she switched off her light.

Lucy was lying awake in the darkness after her parents had gone downstairs, thinking about how Thomas was coming to stay with them in two days' time because it was half-term. Dad was going to collect him in the car and, on the way back, they were stopping off to collect Grandpa too. Grandpa was Dad's father, which meant he was Thomas's grandfather as well. Their grandmother had died several years ago so Grandpa lived on his own now, which Dad said was the reason he tended to be quite grumpy. Having Thomas *and* Grandpa in the house at the same time should be interesting, Lucy thought.

Lucy was just turning over to go to sleep when she heard a noise coming from her sister's room. It sounded like Izzy was out of bed and walking around.

Lucy got up and went into Izzy's room to find that the window was open and Izzy was standing staring out of it, looking upset.

'What's wrong?' Lucy asked her.

'The tooth fairy just came and took my tooth away, but she didn't leave me anything,' Izzy answered.

'Don't be silly!' Lucy said, shutting the window. 'There's no such thing as—' She broke off, remembering that she wasn't meant to tell Izzy that there was no such thing as fairies. 'Your tooth must still be under your pillow. Let me have a look.'

'It's NOT under my pillow,' Izzy snapped angrily. 'I told you! A fairy just came and took it away in a little sack. Fairies are meant to leave you a coin for your tooth, but this one didn't.'

As Lucy searched under her sister's pillow, they heard footsteps on the stairs and their mother came into the room.

'What's going on?' Mum asked.

Izzy repeated the story to her mother, who knelt down to search under the bed for the missing tooth while Lucy continued to feel under the pillow and inside the pillow-slip in case the tooth had got stuck there.

After the search had revealed nothing, Lucy couldn't help laughing. 'Maybe a fairy really did come and take her tooth after all!' Though she didn't truly believe that.

Her mum was giving her a long look. 'You wouldn't know anything about this disappearing tooth, would you, Lucy?'

'Hey, it wasn't me!' Lucy protested.

'I just told you – it was a fairy,' Izzy said crossly. 'I *saw* her! She was wearing a gold sparkly dress and she had a little spoon that she used to scoop up my tooth.'

'You must have been dreaming,' Lucy said, grinning.

'No, I wasn't!'

'How about you both go back to bed now and we'll have another look for this tooth in the morning,' Mum suggested.

'Mummy, the tooth is GONE!' Izzy screeched at the top of her voice. 'You're not even listening to me!'

Izzy could get quite stroppy when she wanted – which always amused Lucy because most of the time Izzy was the one in the family who all the grown-ups seemed to think was a complete angel.

'That's enough shouting,' Mum said firmly. 'Back to bed now – both of you.'

Lucy and Izzy went back to bed, but neither of them could sleep. After a while, Lucy could hear her sister talking to herself in her room and she decided to go and listen. Sometimes Izzy had long conversations with her dolls and her teddies, which Lucy thought were hilarious.

This time, though, Izzy seemed to be talking to totally imaginary people. As Lucy stood in the doorway watching, Izzy was sitting up in bed talking very seriously to the air in front of her.

'But that's terrible! Does your fairy queen know? . . . Really? . . . Well, yes, I think I could give you a description . . .' She suddenly stopped as she noticed Lucy. 'Lucy,' she whispered, 'you'll never guess what! That fairy who took my tooth was a bad fairy. Goldie and Bonnie were meant to collect it – not her.'

'Goldie and Bonnie?' Lucy moved closer to her sister. 'Who are they?'

'The *proper* tooth fairies, of course!' Izzy pointed with one finger of each hand to two spots in the air directly in front of her. 'They're right here!'

'I can't see anything,' Lucy said. 'Stop making things up, Izzy.'

'I'm not making things up!' Izzy seemed to pause to listen, then she turned back to Lucy and frowned. 'Goldie says you can't

see them because you don't believe in fairies.'

'Too right I don't!' Lucy said, noticing that the curtains were drawn back and Izzy's window was open again. It was raining outside and the window sill was getting wet. 'You've got to stop opening this, Izzy,' she said as she went over to close it for a second time.

'It's not me that keeps opening it – it's the fairies! Leave it or they won't be able to get out.' Izzy stopped to listen to her invisible friends again, before adding, 'Oh, can you? That's OK then.'

'What's OK?' Lucy asked.

'I wasn't talking to you – I was talking to *them*. Bonnie says they can open the window themselves quite easily, so not to worry. Tooth fairies are very good at opening windows, she says. She says it's one of their main areas of exper . . . exper . . .' She paused for a moment as if she was listening again. 'Expert-*ise!*' she finished.

Lucy was surprised that Izzy knew such a big word.

'Bonnie says they have to practise opening and closing human windows a lot before they get sent on their first job,' Izzy continued. She was looking towards the window now, saying, 'Oh, please don't go yet!'

'I've got to go back to bed,' Lucy said. 'Izzy, are you just pretending that your tooth's gone missing so you can play this silly—' But she didn't finish her sentence because, as she watched, the window latch was lifting up and the window was opening – all by itself.

Izzy was waving now. 'See you tomorrow!' She turned to her sister and added, 'They

said they're coming back tomorrow when you're not here. They want to speak to me some more, but you're putting them off.'

'How am I putting them off?' Lucy demanded.

'Goldie says that children who don't believe in fairies make fairies get goose-bumps. She and Bonnie can't stay in the same room as you for very long or they get all shivery.'

'Your fairies sound silly to me,' Lucy said crossly.

'I thought you didn't believe fairies were real.'

'I don't!'

'Well, how can they be silly then?' Izzy challenged.

And from outside the window, Lucy was almost sure she heard the sound of a tiny high-pitched giggle.

The following day, Lucy's mum asked her again if she knew anything about Izzy's missing tooth.

'She's playing some sort of pretend game to do with a fairy stealing it,' Lucy said. 'I reckon she's probably hidden it somewhere herself.'

'Well, just so long as Thomas didn't put *you* up to taking it,' Mum said. 'I heard you giggling with him on the phone yesterday and it did occur to me that—'

'It wasn't me, Mum!' Lucy protested.

'And Thomas doesn't even know about it.'

That night, when it was time to go to bed, Lucy told Izzy what their mum had said. 'She thought *I* might have taken your tooth!'

'But that's silly,' Izzy said. 'That bad fairy took my tooth. I told Mummy that.' She looked thoughtful for a moment, then added, 'Mummy *says* she believes in fairies, but sometimes I don't think she *really* does at all.'

Lucy was sure that their mum didn't truly believe in fairies, but she didn't say that. 'Do you think that fairy will bring your tooth back?' she asked instead. 'Because if she doesn't, you won't get a coin for it, will you?'

'That's why I want to help Goldie and

Bonnie catch her,' Izzy said. 'When they come back tonight I'm going to describe her to them.'

Lucy couldn't help being curious about what was going to happen in her sister's room that night, even though she was still almost certain that this whole fairy business was just another of Izzy's make-believe games. The only difference was that until last night she had been *completely* certain of it, whereas now . . .

Soon after she'd gone to bed, Lucy heard Izzy talking to someone in her room. Their mum and dad were downstairs watching a film on the television so Lucy knew they wouldn't be coming upstairs for a while yet. Lucy crept out of bed and quietly opened Izzy's bedroom door. She was *almost* sure that fairies didn't exist, but there *was* that thing that had happened

with the window last night ... After all, windows didn't normally open all by themselves, did they? And what about the giggle she had heard? It had sounded just like the sort of giggle a fairy might make ...

This time, when she entered her sister's room, Izzy wasn't talking to thin air.

There, hovering a little way above Izzy's bed, were two fairies. Lucy gasped out loud when she saw them – and Izzy and the fairies turned to look at her.

'She can see us now,' one of the fairies said as Lucy moved closer.

The fairy was dressed in a

short, floaty yellow dress that had sparkly bits around the hem. She had a thick mop of long, curly, reddish-brown hair and bright green eyes. The other fairy, whose face looked gentler, had a short neat blonde bob and blue eyes. She was wearing a simple white dress and she was holding a miniature notepad and a little gold pencil.

'Hello,' the fairy in the white dress said shyly. 'I'm Bonnie.'

'I'm Goldie,' the other one put in quickly. 'It's amazing what a little bit of doubt can do, isn't it?' she added, grinning.

'What do you mean?' Lucy asked shakily.

'Doubt about fairies! Last night you were certain we were make-believe, so you couldn't see us. But tonight you've started to doubt your own judgement and here we are! Oh, well . . . I suppose we'd better

19

interview you too, since you can see us now. Could you get into bed beside your sister, please?'

Still dazed, Lucy did as she was told. As Izzy moved along a bit to make room for her, Izzy's teddy fell out of bed with a bump.

'He'll have to come back. We haven't finished interviewing him yet,' Goldie said sharply. 'He was in bed with you last night, Izzy, so he's an important witness.'

Izzy quickly reached out of bed and picked up her teddy bear.

Lucy felt her mouth drop open. 'I must be dreaming,' she murmured.

'Do we *look* like dream fairies to you? We're *tooth* fairies and that means that in order to see us you have to be wide awake.

Now pay attention, Teddy,' Goldie added crossly to Izzy's toy bear, who did have a very dopey look on his face.

'I just can't believe this!' Lucy said in amazement. 'I can't believe there really is such a thing as the tooth fairy.'

'Tooth *fairies*,' Goldie corrected her. 'There are a lot more of us than just one!' Goldie quickly told Lucy what the two fairies had already told Izzy – that they had been sent by their fairy queen to find out what had happened the previous night. 'We need to find the fairy who stole Izzy's tooth,' Goldie explained, 'because she's already stolen lots of other teeth from the children in our sector—'

'Your *sector*?' Lucy queried.

'That's right. Tooth fairies always work in pairs and each pair covers a particular sector. Bonnie and I collect teeth from all

the houses in the sector *you* live in, but for the last few weeks, whenever we've arrived to collect a tooth, it's already been taken. None of the children has seen the fairy who took it – until last night. That's why we've come back to question Izzy, to see if we can get a description that will help us.'

'I thought it was mums and dads who took children's teeth and replaced them with coins,' Lucy said. 'I even *saw* my mum come into my room to do it once!'

'Oh, well . . .' Goldie looked a bit shifty all of a sudden. 'That's because we play a trick on the mums and dads, you see.'

'A trick?' Lucy and Izzy said together.

'That's right. You see, a lot of grown-ups don't believe in fairies, so they think that if their children leave a tooth under the pillow, no fairy will really come and take it. And they don't want their children to be disappointed, so they come and take the tooth and put a coin there, which they pretend is from us.'

'But what really happens,' Bonnie continued, 'is that if we know a mum or dad is going to interfere like that – and nearly all of them do – then *we* come and take the tooth away *before* the mum or dad does, and we leave a false fairy tooth in its place for the mums and dads to exchange for their coin. *We* leave a gift too, of course, but not under your pillow.'

'What sort of gift?' Izzy asked.

'Something good for the next day,' Goldie said. 'It might not be a big thing. It might just be a little thing. But if you look out for it, you're bound to spot it.'

'What sort of thing?' Izzy wanted to know.

'Well . . . one time we collected a tooth

from a little girl who loved ice cream,' Bonnie said. 'So the next morning an ice-cream van was in the park when she went there with her dad. That ice-cream van wasn't usually in the park in the mornings – normally it was only there in the afternoons – but we made the driver decide to change his route that day.'

'A little boy who left us his tooth found a book in the library that he'd been wanting to read for ages but couldn't afford to buy,' Goldie said.

'One girl saw a whole lot of baby rabbits when she was out walking in the country with her grandma – that made her really happy,' Bonnie added.

'Something good always happens the next day to children who leave us their teeth,' Goldie finished. 'Only now, all the teeth are getting stolen, which is terrible,

because it means we can't take them back to Fairyland to make them into—'

'*Goldie!*' Bonnie warned her sharply.

Goldie put her hand over her mouth in alarm.

'We're not allowed to tell humans what we do with all the teeth we collect,' Bonnie explained quickly.

'Oh, please tell us!' Izzy begged. 'We won't tell anyone else, will we, Lucy?'

'We *can't* tell you,' Bonnie replied. 'And we really must get on with this interview now. First, I'd better write down the names of all the witnesses. It's Izzy, Lucy and Teddy, right?'

'Well, my *proper* name is Isobel,' Izzy pointed out. 'And I've got three teddies.

This one's proper name is Fat Bear. Not that it really matters, I suppose.'

'Oh, but it *does* matter!' Bonnie exclaimed, carefully writing down their names in sparkly gold handwriting.

'Our fairy queen likes everything to be done properly, you see,' Goldie explained. 'She says it's very important that tooth fairies do everything properly because they have such an important job. That's why we can't go around acting all fluttery and scatterbrained like the other fairies.'

'Like *what* other fairies?' Lucy asked curiously.

'All the other fairies besides tooth fairies! Take flower fairies for instance – they can be very fluttery, especially if it's a breezy day and there's a lot of pollen in the air. Then there are book fairies. They're less fluttery and more sensible like us, because they have

to stay indoors a lot and look after all those books. But they still don't work as hard as we do, because books aren't always falling out at unexpected moments the way teeth are. As for dream fairies, well, they go around with their heads in the clouds all day long!'

'I've seen other fairies a few times,' Izzy said. 'Once I saw one on my window ledge.'

'I expect that was a flower fairy,' Bonnie said. 'Flower fairies spend a lot of time checking people's window ledges to see if anyone's left them any chocolate.'

'Do fairies like chocolate then?' Lucy asked in surprise.

'All fairies *love* chocolate!' Goldie replied. 'Though *our* fairy queen makes us brush our teeth straight away after we eat it. Flower fairies don't have to, and their teeth aren't nearly as shiny and white as ours.' As she spoke, she pulled something out of a pocket

in her dress, which Lucy and Izzy immediately saw was a tiny gold toothbrush.

'Is it a *magic* toothbrush?' Izzy asked in an awed voice, because the bristles seemed to be sparkling.

'Of course it is!' Goldie said, laughing as if she thought the idea of a fairy toothbrush *not* being magical was extremely silly. 'Now then . . .' She waved the brush in the air for silence before beginning the interview with her first question. 'Isobel, can you describe the fairy you saw removing your tooth from under your pillow last night?'

'Well . . . she definitely had on a sparkly gold dress,' Izzy answered, still staring at Goldie's toothbrush. 'And I think her hair was dark brown – like Lucy's.'

'Long or short?' Goldie asked.

'Sort of shoulder length, I think.'

'Curly or straight?'

'Straight, I think. Or maybe a little bit wavy.'

'What colour eyes?'

'I didn't really notice her eyes.'

Goldie turned to Lucy. 'What about you? Did *you* see what colour her eyes were?'

Lucy shook her head. 'I didn't see her at all.'

'Lucy didn't even *believe* in fairies until tonight,' Izzy reminded them.

Frowning, Goldie turned to Izzy's teddy for help. 'Did *you* see this fairy, Fat Bear?'

Everyone stared at the toy bear, and Lucy and Izzy found themselves half expecting him to suddenly come to life and start talking.

That didn't happen, but Goldie seemed to be getting some sort of answer from him, just the same. 'I see,' she said gravely, after listening intently for a minute or so.

'Well, that's very helpful. Thank you, Fat Bear.' She turned back to the others. 'Fat Bear didn't see the colour of her eyes either, but he noticed that the fairy in question was wearing red boots. She actually trod on him on her way to the pillow, which is what woke him up.'

'Did my teddy *really* tell you that?' Izzy asked in disbelief.

'Toys can't speak out loud, but fairies can listen to their thoughts,' Goldie explained. 'And his thoughts are telling me that the boots were red and shiny with high heels and that the fairy trod on his tummy and didn't even say, "Excuse me".'

'A rude fairy with red shiny boots!' Bonnie had put down her gold pencil and was staring at Goldie in alarm.

Goldie nodded. 'I know. It does sound like her, doesn't it?'

'Like *who*?' Lucy and Izzy demanded together.

'Like a tooth fairy we know called Precious,' Goldie told them. 'She used to live with us in Tooth-fairy Land but she got banished a while ago for being bad. Nobody's seen her since. We thought it might be a flower fairy or a dream fairy who was taking the teeth, but it's been her all along! She must want to stop us using them to make—'

'*GOLDIE!*' Bonnie bellowed.

Goldie quickly clamped her hand over her mouth again.

'Come on,' Bonnie told her impatiently. 'We'd better get back and report our findings to the fairy queen.'

'Maybe we can help you catch this bad fairy,' Lucy said, because she had suddenly had an idea.

'How?' Goldie and Bonnie asked together, pausing in mid wing-flap.

'I've still got nearly all my baby teeth locked away inside my jewellery box,' Lucy told them. 'If you wanted, I could leave them under my pillow to make Precious come back again. Then you could wait for her in my bedroom and catch her.'

'That wouldn't work,' Goldie said quickly. 'Precious would pick up our scents.'

'Your *scents*?'

'A fairy can always smell when another fairy's nearby,' Bonnie explained. 'But there might be another way we could use your teeth to catch Precious. We'll speak to our fairy queen and come back tomorrow night to tell you what she says.'

And with that, the two fairies flew out of the window and vanished.

3

The following afternoon, Thomas and Grandpa arrived having already had an argument in the car.

'It wasn't just Thomas's fault,' Lucy's dad was saying to her mum as Lucy walked into the kitchen that evening. 'Of course Thomas is excited because he hasn't seen me for a whole month and he's got lots to tell me. But you know my father! He had plenty to say too – including the fact that in *his* day children were seen and not heard! He told Thomas off for interrupting him,

so after that Thomas made a point of interrupting him even more. I did suggest that since they both wanted to talk so badly, they should try having a conversation with each other and leave me to concentrate on driving – but that idea went down like a lead balloon!'

Just then, Thomas hobbled into the room behind Lucy, leaning heavily on Grandpa's walking stick and doing a very good imitation of a grumpy old man. 'Spare the rod and spoil the child, that's what I say!' he growled, shaking the stick at Lucy and pulling a very Grandpa-like face.

They all laughed, but then they heard Grandpa shouting that his stick was missing, and Dad sighed and said, 'You'd better go and give it back to him, Thomas.'

Five minutes later Grandpa and Thomas could be heard arguing loudly again because they wanted to watch different things on TV.

'Thank goodness it's nearly bedtime,' Mum said, sounding tired. 'Come on, Lucy. I've already made up the spare bed for Grandpa, but I need you to come and help me set up Thomas's camp bed in your room.'

Later, when the children had gone to bed, Lucy waited until her parents had gone back downstairs before telling Thomas everything that had happened the previous night. When she had finished telling him all about Goldie and Bonnie and the bad fairy called Precious, who had stolen Izzy's tooth, she added excitedly, 'So we were wrong about tooth fairies not being real. It just *seems* like it's your parents who take your tooth away!'

But Thomas responded by laughing at

her. 'Nice try, Lucy, but I'm not that much of a sucker.'

'I'm not trying to trick you, Thomas!' she protested. 'Fairies *are* real! If you believe in them, even just a little bit, then you'll be able to see them too. They're coming back tonight after they've had a talk with their fairy queen.'

'In your dreams, Lucy,' Thomas grunted, turning on to his side to go to sleep.

Lucy stayed awake for as long as she could, waiting for Goldie and Bonnie to return. But eventually, when they still didn't come, she found that she couldn't keep her eyes open any longer.

It was the middle of the night and Lucy was sound asleep when Goldie and Bonnie finally flew in through her bedroom window, accompanied by a third fairy, whose wings were much bigger and shinier

than theirs. The new fairy wore shimmery white trousers (that were exactly the same colour as the whitest, glossiest tooth enamel), a matching white jacket and dainty white boots. Her long golden hair was coiled up on top of her head and she wore a gold crown made from little tooth-shaped gold droplets. In one hand she held a golden toothbrush with bristles that sparkled and, as she flew across the room, she waved the toothbrush over Lucy like a wand, releasing a shower of golden dust over Lucy's head.

The dust seemed to be a waking spell because, as it touched her skin, Lucy opened her eyes and was instantly alert.

The fairy smiled at her, then flew off to wake up Izzy.

'Goldie! Bonnie!' Lucy gasped as she spotted the two fairies hovering above the camp bed where Thomas was sleeping.

'Who's that?' they asked, peering at him curiously.

'My brother – he doesn't believe in fairies so there's no point waking him up,' Lucy said. In fact, she had a feeling it would be better *not* to wake him, judging by the way he had reacted when she'd told him about the fairies. 'I'm so glad you came back,' she added. 'I was starting to think you weren't going to!'

'Queen Eldora wanted to make sure all the grown-ups in the house were asleep

before we came,' Bonnie explained. 'That's why we're so late.'

'Queen Eldora?'

'Our fairy queen. We told her about your teeth and she decided to come and meet you. She was the one who woke you up just now.'

'*That* was Queen Eldora?'

'That's right. She's fetching Izzy so she can interview you both herself.'

'You tooth fairies seem to have a bit of a thing about interviewing people,' Lucy said, yawning.

Goldie and Bonnie giggled. 'Interviews and meetings are Queen Eldora's favourite things,' Goldie told her.

Izzy came into the room then, followed by the fairy queen, who was lighting up the darkness like a torch with the glow from her shining wings.

'I am Queen Eldora, queen of the tooth fairies,' she said. 'But I expect you already know that.'

Lucy nodded and Izzy couldn't help blurting out, 'You don't *look* much like a fairy queen.'

Queen Eldora laughed. 'Did you expect me to be dressed up in a big frilly frock, waving a wand about all over the place?'

'I don't know exactly,' Izzy replied. 'But *my* fairy-queen dress is pink with silver stars on it. And *my* wand has a flashing light and it plays a tune when you press the button.'

Queen Eldora laughed again. 'Well, tooth fairies have magic toothbrushes to wave instead of wands.'

'*I* think you look really cool,' Lucy told her quickly.

The fairy queen smiled at Lucy. 'Thank

you. Now . . . I hear you have some teeth that you wish to give us. Is that correct?'

Lucy nodded. 'I didn't believe in fairies before, so that's why I've still got them,' she explained.

'Thomas said she should make a necklace out of them,' Izzy put in, 'but Lucy didn't want to.'

'I should think not,' the fairy queen said. 'Using teeth to make jewellery is a terrible waste.' Lucy noticed that, although Queen Eldora had tooth-shaped droplets in her crown and a trouser suit and boots that were exactly the same colour as tooth enamel, she wasn't wearing any real teeth as part of her outfit.

'What *should* teeth be used for then?' she asked curiously.

'That's for fairies to know and children to guess at,' Queen Eldora replied briskly.

'Though if you help us, we might tell you.'

'Of course we'll help you,' Lucy said. 'I'll get you the teeth right now – there are six of them!'

As Lucy got out of bed and went over to her dressing table, Queen Eldora turned to Goldie and Bonnie and asked in a teacherish voice, 'So what sort of teeth do you expect these to be?'

'Incisors!' the two younger fairies chorused immediately.

'Excellent!' the fairy queen said, smiling at them. 'I can see that you have both been paying attention at your tooth-fairy lectures.'

Lucy unlocked her jewellery box and took out a little blue pouch, which she brought back to her bed and carefully tipped up.

42

'Don't let any teeth touch your pillow,' Queen Eldora warned her.

'Why not?' Lucy asked.

'Everything will be explained to you later, but first I must examine these teeth,' the fairy queen replied, flying down on to Lucy's bed where she touched each of Lucy's teeth in turn with the bristles of her fairy toothbrush. Each time she did so, the handle of the brush lit up. 'These are very fine teeth,' Queen Eldora pronounced when she had finished. 'They could be of great use to us.'

'How—?' Lucy started to ask, but she was interrupted by Izzy.

'Lucy, look!'

And that's when Lucy saw that Thomas had woken up and that he was lying very still on his camp bed, his eyes wide open, watching her.

4

Before Lucy could speak, Thomas sat up in bed and said, 'You are totally mad, you know that?'

'Wait!' Lucy gasped as Queen Eldora flew away from the bed towards the window, beckoning Goldie and Bonnie to follow her. 'He can't hurt you! He doesn't believe in fairies so he can't even see you!'

But Thomas was already getting out of bed, looking like he wanted to join in the fun even though he couldn't actually see the fairies. 'Who says I don't believe in fairies?'

he teased, grinning as he watched Lucy quickly scoop up all her baby teeth from the bed. 'These are tooth fairies, aren't they? Well, tell them I've got something for them!'

'Where's he going?' Izzy whispered as their brother left the room.

Over on the window ledge, Queen Eldora, Goldie and Bonnie were all starting to shiver, despite the fact that it wasn't cold, and Lucy suddenly remembered what Izzy had told her about fairies getting goosebumps when they stayed in the same room as a child who didn't believe in them.

'Thomas has been here the whole time, so how come you haven't got shivery until now?' she asked them.

'*All* children believe in fairies when they're asleep,' the fairy queen answered matter-of-factly. 'We'll come back to-morrow night, Lucy. Keep those teeth safe until then.'

'We will!' Lucy and Izzy called out together as the three fairies flew off into the night sky and disappeared.

As Izzy rushed to the window to look out, Lucy went to lock the teeth back inside her jewellery box. She was just returning the key to the top drawer, where she kept it hidden under her socks, when Thomas came back into the room with something in his hand.

'Here you are, tooth fairies!' he called out to the room in general. 'A present for you!' He was holding the jar with Grandpa's false teeth

inside it, which Grandpa always kept by his bed during the night. He took the jar over to the window and put it down on the outside window ledge.

Izzy immediately started giggling.

'Thomas, you'd better take that back,' Lucy said, but she couldn't help laughing a bit too.

Suddenly the landing light went on.

Lucy quickly drew the curtains shut to hide Grandpa's dentures, just as their father appeared in the doorway.

'What's going on in here?' Their dad looked dazed and bleary-eyed and he clearly wasn't pleased to have been woken up. He frowned even more when he saw Izzy. 'What are you doing in here, young lady?' As Izzy fled back to her own room, he scowled at Thomas and Lucy as they hurriedly got back into bed too. 'Now be quiet and go back to sleep, both of you!'

After their father had gone back to bed and the house was silent again, Lucy whispered, 'What are we going to do about Grandpa's teeth? Dad might hear us if we try and take them back now.'

'We'll take them back in the morning,' Thomas said.

'We'd better get them in from the window ledge then. You go and get them, Thomas. You're the one who put them there!'

'I'll do it in the morning,' Thomas muttered, closing his eyes.

But Lucy was too worried to leave Grandpa's dentures outside all night so she got out of bed, went over to the window and pulled back the curtains. That was when she saw a fairy in a gold dress and red

boots, watching her from a spot in the night air a short distance away. And the fairy was balancing the jar of dentures on her head!

'Precious!' Lucy gasped, recognizing her immediately from Izzy's description.

'Thanks for the present!' Precious called back, grinning at her mischievously.

'They're not for you!' Lucy hissed, at which point Thomas got out of bed and came over to the window too.

'Who are you talking to?' he grunted.

'*Her!*' Lucy replied, pointing at Precious.

But all Thomas saw was the jar of false teeth floating in mid-air ... except that false teeth *couldn't* float in mid-air ... He gaped in disbelief at the jar, which was now dancing around in the moonlight. Something had to be holding it up, only whatever it was seemed to be invisible ... And the only invisible thing he could think of was the thing that Lucy had told him about – the thing he had refused to believe in until now ...

And all of a sudden – the second that tiny bit of doubt entered his mind – Thomas could see Precious too.

'Give my regards to Queen Eldora, won't you?' Precious called out, as she gave them a cheeky wave and flew out of sight.

'What are we going to do?' Lucy gasped.

But Thomas was too stunned to speak.

*

At least Thomas believed in fairies now, Lucy thought, but that still didn't solve the problem of Grandpa's teeth.

Lucy and Thomas both acted dumb the next morning when Grandpa came downstairs demanding to know who had taken his dentures. He looked much older and frailer without his teeth in, and Lucy felt terrible. But she knew no one would believe them if they tried to explain what had happened.

Thomas wasn't looking like he felt terrible at all. He looked as if he found the sight of Grandpa without his dentures extremely funny. Izzy, who knew nothing about what had happened after she'd gone back to bed, just looked surprised. Dad was watching all their faces, Lucy noticed, and he seemed to decide immediately who was responsible.

'Thomas, do you know anything about this?' he asked.

Thomas immediately stopped smirking. 'Oh, so you're just assuming *I* must have done it, are you?' he answered back.

'Thomas—'

'I haven't got his rotten old teeth, OK?' Thomas snapped, pushing back his chair and knocking some cutlery on to the floor

with his elbow as he jumped up. 'Have I, Lucy?'

'Lucy, do you know anything about this?' Mum asked immediately.

But before Lucy could answer, Grandpa growled, 'That boy needs a good hiding, that's what. And if I don't get my teeth back right now—' He was lifting up his walking stick as if he intended to hit Thomas with it.

'Father, I think you'd better let me handle this,' Dad interrupted, grabbing the end of the stick before it could do any damage. 'Thomas, if you won't answer my question then I think you'd better go to your room.'

'I don't *have* a room here!' Thomas pointed out stubbornly. 'Remember?' And before anyone could say anything else, he had stormed out.

'Don't worry, we'll get your dentures back,' Mum said in an attempt to soothe their grandfather. She looked at Lucy again. 'Lucy, if you know where Grandpa's teeth are, I suggest you tell us right now.'

'I don't know exactly where they are,' Lucy answered truthfully, 'and neither does Thomas. But I promise we'll try and find out . . .' She quickly left the table and went upstairs to join her brother, knowing that they didn't have long before her parents came to interrogate them some more.

Thomas was sitting cross-legged on the camp bed, his face red with anger. 'It's not fair! Dad always thinks everything is my fault. He never blames you or Izzy!'

'Thomas, this *is* your fault!' Lucy pointed out impatiently. 'And Dad only picked on you because you were laughing, and that was really mean because this isn't

54

very funny for Grandpa, is it? We've just *got* to get those teeth back!'

'I don't see how,' Thomas grunted.

'You could always try being very nice to *me*!' a little voice piped up from behind them, and Lucy and Thomas turned to see Precious standing on the window sill, watching them. She was wearing a little red cape over her gold dress, and the same

red boots she'd worn the night before. 'If you want your grandfather's teeth back, I can bring them to you,' she offered. 'Though I'd want something in return, of course.' She laughed at Thomas, whose mouth had fallen open. 'That's right, you silly boy! You *weren't* dreaming last night. Fairies *are* real!'

Lucy found her voice at last. 'Precious, please bring back Grandpa's teeth. If you do, I know just what we can give you in return.'

'Oh?'

'*Chocolate!* Goldie and Bonnie said that all fairies love it, and we could get you loads! You just need to tell us what kind you like best and—'

'I do like chocolate,' Precious interrupted, licking her lips at the thought, 'but that's not what I want. You see . . . a

little bird I know flew past here last night and saw you showing some lovely baby teeth to Queen Eldora. You *have* still got them, haven't you?'

Lucy gulped. 'Yes, but—'

'Good! Let me see them then!'

Lucy had no choice but to do what Precious said. Nervously, she went over and unlocked her jewellery box, tipping the teeth out on to the palm of her hand before bringing them over to show the excited fairy.

'Lovely,' Precious gasped, eyeing the teeth greedily. 'Give them to me now and I'll go and get your grandfather's teeth straight away.'

'No way!' Thomas put in swiftly. 'If you want Lucy's teeth, you'll have to give us Grandpa's first. Otherwise, how do we know you'll keep your word?'

'Fairies *always* keep their word!' Precious replied a little haughtily.

'*Good* fairies might,' Thomas said.

Precious scowled at him. 'Very well,' she snapped. 'I'll come back tonight with the false teeth and you'd better have all six of these real teeth here waiting for me. But if you tell any of the other fairies about this, the deal's off!'

After she'd gone, Lucy and Thomas sat down on Lucy's bed feeling too dazed to speak.

'It was even weirder seeing a fairy in broad daylight,' Thomas finally murmured.

'I know,' Lucy agreed.

'So what are we going to do? Are you really going to give her your teeth?'

'I think I'll have to. I know I promised the tooth-fairy queen that I'd give them to *her*, but if I don't do what Precious

says, she won't give back Grandpa's
dentures.'

Thomas was looking thoughtful. 'What
about if we give Precious the teeth and take
back Grandpa's dentures, but then we stop
Precious getting away afterwards?'

'How can we stop her? All she has to do
is fly out of the window and she'll be out of
reach.'

'Out of reach of our *hands* maybe,'
Thomas agreed. 'But there are other ways
to catch a fairy.'

'Like what?' Lucy asked, puzzled.

'Well, remember how Dad was going to
take me fishing last time I came here, but
in the end we didn't go?'

Lucy nodded. The fishing trip had
been the cause of yet another family
argument. It was Thomas who hadn't
wanted to go, Lucy remembered, after

Lucy had said that she'd like to try fishing too, and their dad had suggested turning the fishing trip into an outing for the whole family. Mum had made up a picnic for them all and then, at the last minute, Thomas had announced that he didn't want to go and had shut himself in the spare room.

'Has Dad still got that fishing net in the garage, do you know?' Thomas asked now. 'The one with the long handle?'

'I think so,' Lucy replied. 'Why? Do you think we could use *that* to catch Precious?'

'Well, it's worth a try, isn't it?' Thomas said. 'Come on!'

On their way downstairs, Lucy's mum stopped them to ask where they were going.

'We're just going outside to fetch something,' Lucy told her.

'I see,' Mum replied, and Lucy immediately wished she hadn't spoken. Mum clearly thought she knew *exactly* what they were going outside to fetch, and now she would expect them to return to the house with Grandpa's missing dentures.

It was going to be a long day, Lucy thought gloomily, as she followed her brother out to the garage.

5

Lucy thought that the day would never end, but eventually it did – earlier than usual, because her parents sent all the children to bed straight after their evening meal. Although Lucy and Thomas continued to say that they didn't know the whereabouts of Grandpa's missing teeth – and Izzy truly didn't know anything – their parents clearly thought otherwise.

Grandpa had sat hunched up in the armchair in front of the television for most of the day and all his meals had had to be

soft ones because he couldn't chew properly. He refused even to look at the children, who he was sure were responsible for his missing dentures.

'I wish we could tell them the truth,' Lucy kept saying to Thomas.

'They'd only get even madder at us because they'd think we were making it up,' Thomas said.

'Even if we get Grandpa's teeth back we're still going to be in trouble,' Lucy said gloomily. 'They're still going to think we were the ones who took them. Maybe I should've given my teeth to Precious this morning like she wanted. She said she'd bring Grandpa's dentures back straight away then, didn't she?'

'That's what she *said*,' Thomas replied. 'But I don't trust her.'

The two children had decided to wait

until bedtime before telling Izzy anything, mainly because Izzy wasn't as good as Lucy and Thomas were at keeping secrets from their parents.

'*Precious* took Grandpa's teeth?' Izzy gasped in disbelief, when Lucy finally crept into her room and told her the whole story.

Lucy quickly explained how she and Thomas were planning to catch Precious when she came to exchange Grandpa's dentures for Lucy's teeth that night. 'We've got Dad's fishing net and a big cardboard box all ready,' Lucy said. 'We've made holes in the lid so she can breathe and we'll hand her over to the other fairies as soon as they get here.'

'I want to come and see you catch her,' Izzy said.

'You can't,' Lucy replied. 'If Mum and

Dad find out you're not in bed, it'll ruin everything.'

'They won't find out! I'll put my pillow down my bed to make it look like me,' Izzy said, getting up and quickly rearranging her bed. Although it wasn't dark outside yet, it would be soon, and Lucy had to admit that if her mum or dad just looked in on Izzy briefly from the doorway, they were likely to be fooled.

'Come on then,' Lucy said, and the two girls went back to Lucy's room together.

'Actually,' Thomas said, after Lucy and Izzy had joined him, 'having Izzy here as well isn't a bad idea. Precious will only expect there to be two of us, so we'll leave the curtains open and Izzy can hide behind one of them with the fishing net. Then, when Precious has handed over Grandpa's teeth and she's flying away again, Izzy can jump out with the net and surprise her as she leaves through the window.'

'But what if she's too fast for me to catch?' Izzy said, frowning.

Thomas looked around the room, then picked up Lucy's notepad and started to rip out the pages, crunching them up into paper balls. 'You can practise before she gets here,' he told Izzy. 'Try and catch these when I throw them out the window.' He went to fetch the net, which they had hidden in Lucy's wardrobe.

But Izzy wasn't very good at catching the paper balls in the net and they had just stopped practising and were trying to think up a new plan, when they heard a noise on the landing.

'We'd better shut the curtains! And you can hide behind them, Izzy!' Lucy hissed,

pulling the curtains shut in front of both
Izzy and the fishing net, before jumping
back into bed herself.

One of the grown-ups had just gone into
the bathroom, and the children waited in
silence until they heard the bathroom door
opening again and whoever it was going
back downstairs. Then Lucy and Thomas
got out of bed, whispering to Izzy that it
was safe for her to come out now. But when
they went over to the window and drew
back the curtains, Izzy wasn't there.

Thomas cried out and Lucy felt like her
legs were about to give way under her.

That was when they saw that Grandpa's
jar of false teeth was sitting on the window
ledge and that Precious herself was
hovering in the air, just out of reach. She
was holding the long handle of the fishing
net in the middle, a bit like a tightrope

walker might hold a pole to help them balance. And, at the net end, Lucy saw a tiny figure trapped inside the mesh, struggling and shouting out for help.

'Izzy?' Lucy gasped, hardly able to believe it. 'Is that *you*?'

'I used some fairy dust to shrink her down to fairy size,' Precious said. 'I saw you practising how you were going to catch *me*, so now I've caught one of *you* instead.

That'll teach you to try and trick me!' And she flew away, taking Izzy with her, leaving Lucy and Thomas staring after her, speechless with shock.

'Thomas, what are we going to do?' Lucy finally blurted.

Thomas's voice sounded hoarse as he gasped, 'I don't know.'

Lucy struggled to think clearly. 'The other fairies will be here soon. They'll help us.' But she still had to fight the urge to run downstairs and tell her parents everything, even though she knew that her parents would never believe her and would either fly into a panic when they realized Izzy was missing or, more likely, assume that the children were playing another trick on them and become even angrier than they'd been about Grandpa's missing teeth.

Lucy couldn't stop trembling, and Thomas refused to move from the window as they waited for the other fairies to return.

'This is all my fault,' Thomas kept saying over and over. 'If I hadn't mucked around with Grandpa's teeth, this would never have happened.' They had removed Grandpa's dentures from the window ledge, but had decided it was best not to risk drawing any attention to themselves by replacing them in Grandpa's room just yet. Instead they had put them out of sight in Lucy's wardrobe.

'I shouldn't have tried to make Izzy be the one to catch Precious,' Thomas added. 'I should have just done it myself.'

Lucy didn't say anything. After all, she had thought it was a good idea for Izzy to jump out and surprise Precious too, hadn't she?

Just then a noise outside made them turn and suddenly Queen Eldora was flying in through the window with Goldie and Bonnie following close behind.

'Thank goodness!' Lucy cried out as the three fairies settled on top of Lucy's dressing table, clearly surprised to see that Thomas was looking at them now. But before Thomas could explain how he had come to believe in fairies so quickly, Lucy blurted out the news that Precious had kidnapped Izzy.

Queen Eldora looked stunned. 'I've never heard of any fairy doing such a terrible thing!'

'She must have done a very quick shrinking spell,' Goldie said.

'Can Izzy be *un*-shrunk again?' Thomas asked anxiously.

Goldie nodded. 'Fairy shrinking spells

never last long if you do them outside Fairyland.'

'I don't understand why Precious is behaving like this,' Bonnie said, sounding upset. 'She knows she'll *never* be able to come home again if she carries on being this bad.'

'The golden pillowcase will never let her through now she's been *this* wicked,' Goldie agreed.

'How do you mean?' Lucy asked. '*What* golden pillowcase?'

Queen Eldora started to speak then. 'Tooth fairies travel in and out of Fairyland via magic fairy pillowcases, which are golden in colour and hang on human washing lines. They are invisible to most humans, of course – only those who believe in fairies can see them. But no fairy can pass through a magic pillowcase unless she has a certain amount of Goodness in her.'

'That's why Precious is stuck here,' Goldie explained. 'Because she's done too many bad things and her Goodness levels have dropped too low.'

'What sort of bad things?' Thomas asked curiously.

'Many different bad things, I'm afraid,' the fairy queen answered. 'And she's never sorry afterwards, which makes it even worse.'

'Once she stole a little girl's favourite doll because she thought the doll's clothes would look nice on *her*,' Bonnie said. 'And then when they didn't fit properly she dumped the doll and all her clothes in a dustbin.'

'Another time she ate all the chocolate icing off the top of a little boy's birthday

cake,' Goldie added. 'He cried when he saw it and his mum was upset too because she'd spent ages decorating it.'

'Once when I was collecting teeth with her we had an argument and she got so cross she shut me inside a drawer and I was stuck there until someone came and opened it the next morning,' Bonnie said, frowning.

'Anyway, she's been banished from Fairyland for as long as it takes for her to become a good enough fairy again,' Goldie told them. 'Only instead of trying to be good, she's been stealing all our teeth – and stopping us from using them to make Goodness!'

'*Goldie!*' Bonnie screeched, and Goldie immediately clamped her hands over her mouth in horror.

'It's all right, Goldie,' the fairy queen

said. 'I think it's time we told Lucy and Thomas our secret.' She turned to the children. 'Tooth fairies use children's teeth to make a magic Goodness dust that we sprinkle about wherever it's needed. It's quite invisible to the human eye, of course.'

'*Goodness dust?*' Thomas and Lucy repeated together.

'That's right,' Queen Eldora replied. 'Goodness dust makes people kinder and more helpful to each other. That's not to say there isn't a lot of human kindness and helpfulness in the world in any case, but by sprinkling the air with Goodness we make people feel even more like helping each other. So you see, Goodness is a very important substance, which is why—'

But she was interrupted by a small brown bird, which had landed on the

window ledge and was now chirping to get their attention.

'Look!' Goldie exclaimed, pointing at it, and Lucy saw that in its beak the little bird was clasping a tiny gold envelope.

'It's from Precious,' Queen Eldora said, opening the letter after the bird had flown away. 'It's addressed to me so she must know I'm visiting you. She says she has sent us one of your sister's giggles to let us know that Izzy is still with her and that she's quite safe.'

'How can she send a *giggle*?' Thomas asked.

Queen Eldora peered further into the envelope, then turned it upside down and shook it. Suddenly it was just as if Izzy was

in the room with them as the sound of her giggling filled the air.

'That's Izzy's giggle all right,' Lucy said, feeling more hopeful as she added, 'If Izzy's having such a good time, Precious can't be *that* bad, can she?'

'She is not completely bad, no,' Queen Eldora agreed, 'but I'm sorry to say that she is bad *enough*! Now . . .' She went back to reading the letter. 'She says that Izzy is safe and she promises not to harm her, but if we want her back, Lucy has to give Precious her pouch of teeth, and this time she mustn't try to trick her. Lucy, she wants you to meet her at six o'clock tomorrow morning out in the garden before anyone else is up. And she says if she smells any other fairies nearby, she won't show herself.' Queen Eldora looked thoughtful. 'I won't be able to send any of my fairies with you

when you go to meet her, but I do have an idea how we can find out where she's hiding – after we've got Izzy back safely, of course.'

'*How?*' Lucy and Thomas asked.

'You must give her the teeth like she says and then, after she tells you where Izzy is, someone must follow her to see where she goes. Since no other fairy will be able to follow her without being detected, I propose that we send you, Lucy. It will mean changing you into a fairy for a little while but—'

'A *fairy?*' Lucy blurted out. 'You mean with wings and everything?'

'Of course! You'll look exactly like a real fairy – but because you're not, Precious won't be able to pick up your fairy scent the way she could with one of us. But are you willing to do this?'

'Of course I'll do it!'

'Excellent!' Queen Eldora smiled at her. 'We'll shrink you down straight away and take you back to Fairyland with us. We shall have to fit you with a suitable pair of wings when we get there, and teach you how to use them, but that shouldn't take long—'

'Hey, what about me?' Thomas suddenly demanded.

Queen Eldora looked at him. 'You wish to be changed into a fairy too?'

Thomas flushed. 'Well, maybe not a fairy exactly, but—'

'There's no need to be embarrassed. We do have fairy boys as well as girls – I'm sure we could find you a pair of wings too if you want to help your sister.'

'I do want to,' Thomas said quickly.

'All right then. We'll take you both back

to Fairyland with us – but first I must perform a spell on your beds so your parents won't see that you've gone.' She waved her magic toothbrush around so that a sprinkling of fairy dust rained down over both the children's beds. Then she flew off into Izzy's room to repeat her spell in there.

'Our beds don't look any different to me,' Lucy said when the fairy queen returned.

'That's because the spell isn't meant for you – it's meant for your parents. If they look in on you while you're gone, they'll see just what they expect to see! Now . . . this spell *is* meant for you . . . I want you to stand together and hold hands . . . that's it . . . now, close your eyes.'

Lucy and Thomas did as they were told and as they stood together with their eyes tightly shut they both felt a strange tingling sensation all over.

'You can look now,' the fairy queen said after a minute or two.

They opened their eyes and found that they were in a completely different room – or at least, that was how it seemed at first. Their heads felt swimmy as they stared at everything in utter amazement. The ceiling was now as far away as the sky and they were standing between two huge, unrecognizable structures, which were actually their beds.

Queen Eldora flew down from the top of Lucy's chest of drawers – which now seemed like a very tall building – and the children saw that she was the same size as they were. Her hair and clothes seemed much brighter than theirs though and, as Lucy gazed at the fairy queen's enormous glowing wings, she wondered if she was going to be given a pair even half as beautiful.

Then Goldie and Bonnie joined them
and the three fairies took hold of the
children's hands and lifted them up.

'Wow!' Thomas shrieked as they shot
out through the window. 'This is so cool! I
feel like Peter Pan!'

'Who's he?' Bonnie and Goldie asked.

'He's a boy in a story, who can fly,' Thomas said, looking down in amazement at their garden, which looked huge now as they flew over it. 'There's a fairy in the story called Tinkerbell. Don't tell me you haven't heard of *her* either!'

'We only know *real* fairies, not make-believe ones,' Goldie told him. But Thomas was no longer paying attention, because they had flown over the fence into their neighbours' garden and there, hanging on the washing line and glowing brightly in the dark, was an enormous gold-coloured pillowcase.

'You mean the entrance to Fairyland has been right next door to us all along?' Lucy exclaimed.

'*One* of the entrances,' Queen Eldora replied. 'There are many other pillowcases just like this one. Golden pillowcases are situated all over the world – wherever children believe in tooth fairies.'

The top end of the pillowcase was open and, once inside, the children found themselves in a gold room that didn't look anything like the inside of a pillowcase. At the far end of the room was a set of gold doors that were closed, but there was a button next to them, which Goldie flew over to and pressed.

'This is where we catch the fairy lift,' Queen Eldora told them. As she spoke, the doors slid open to reveal a floor-to-ceiling curtain of sparkling golden dust.

'That's the Goodness curtain,' Goldie explained. 'We have to fly through that to get to the lift.' And she flew straight into the curtain of dust and vanished.

'The *Goodness* curtain?' Lucy's mouth was hanging open.

'Remember how I told you that no fairy can pass through a golden pillowcase into Fairyland unless she has enough Goodness inside her?' Queen Eldora said. 'Well, that is because the Goodness curtain is present in each pillowcase.'

'So you mean there are *lots* of Goodness curtains?' Lucy asked.

'Oh no! There is only one Goodness curtain, but it is so powerful it can be in many places at once. It appears by magic inside each pillowcase whenever a fairy needs to use it, and it unites all the entrances to Tooth-fairy Land. Once a fairy flies through the Goodness curtain she always arrives in the same place – the fairy lift that takes her home again.'

'Does the Goodness curtain let *children* travel through it into Fairyland then?' Thomas asked.

'If they are shrunken children, yes, though the same Goodness rules apply to children as to fairies,' Queen Eldora told him. 'If you are good enough, it will let you through. Now follow me, please.' And she flew into the curtain and vanished in a white flash of light.

'But what happens if you're *not* good enough?' Thomas asked Bonnie nervously after the fairy queen had gone.

'Nothing will happen except that the Goodness curtain will feel like a solid wall and you'll be stuck on this side of it.'

'Is that what happened to Precious?' Lucy asked.

'Yes.'

'That must have been horrible for her,' Lucy said, frowning. 'Not being able to get home, I mean.'

'Hey, don't go feeling too sorry for her,'

Thomas protested. 'She's just kidnapped our sister, remember. Even *I'd* never do anything as bad as that!'

And reminding himself of that seemed to give him the courage he needed, because he took one step towards the curtain, then another, and suddenly he had disappeared too.

'Come on, Lucy,' Bonnie said, flying towards the curtain herself. 'There's nothing to be afraid of.'

So Lucy followed Bonnie and for a few seconds everything was so bright she couldn't see anything except whiteness. She held her hands up to her eyes to shield them from the glare and when she removed them she found herself in a second room that had shiny gold walls and no windows.

The others were already there waiting for her.

'This is the lift to Fairyland,' Queen Eldora told her. And before Lucy had time to point out that the room seemed far too big to be a lift, it had started to move – though it was difficult to tell in exactly what direction.

Goldie grinned and pressed a button in the wall that made five gold chairs spring up from the floor for them to sit on. 'We can have beds to lie down on too, if you're sleepy,' she said. 'Or if you're hungry, we can order a table with a picnic on it.'

'Is it going to take a really long time to get there then?' Lucy asked in surprise.

'No *real* time at all,' Queen Eldora reassured her. 'Time stops completely while we're in this lift – which is why my fairies often like to have a nap here, or eat a nice meal, because they can do so without using up any time whatsoever.'

'But when do we get to Fairyland?' Thomas asked a little impatiently.

'Whenever we like. All we have to do is say the magic words.'

'*What* magic words?'

The fairy queen smiled. 'If you're that keen to get there, we can say them at once.' She looked at Goldie and Bonnie expectantly.

Goldie and Bonnie linked hands and closed their eyes, and looked very solemn for a few moments before suddenly yelling out at the tops of their voices, '*Are we nearly there yet?*'

Lucy and Thomas both jumped.

'*Those* are the magic words?' Thomas said in disbelief, as the lift abruptly stopped moving.

'They don't work when you're using human transport, of course,' Queen Eldora replied, smiling, 'but they *always* work if you're travelling in a fairy lift!'

'Welcome to Tooth-fairy Land,' Bonnie and Goldie sang out, and the children held their breath as the lift doors slid open.

Nervously, Lucy and Thomas stepped out-side after the two fairies.

They had arrived in what looked like the central square of a fairy town, except that instead of having normal buildings in it, all the houses looked like giant white teeth!

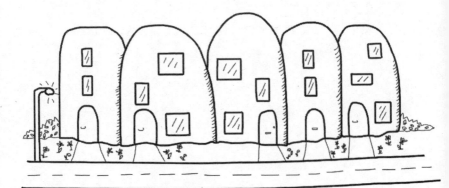

'You don't . . . you don't use *real* teeth to make your houses, do you?' Thomas couldn't help asking, which made Queen Eldora burst out laughing.

'Of course not!' she replied. 'Real teeth are solid in the middle so how could we live inside them?'

'Unless they've gone rotten, of course,' Goldie added, giggling, 'but no fairy would want to live inside a rotten tooth!'

'We build things in the *shape* of teeth wherever we can, that's all,' Queen Eldora explained.

Lucy saw that each of the tooth-shaped houses had a little door and little windows and that they seemed to be arranged in orderly streets leading off from the main square. Some of the houses were tall and thin while others were shorter and fatter. Outside the nearest shorter house there

was a little painted sign saying, 1 Molar Mews. The next street, which had a row of taller houses in it, had a plaque at the end that read, Canine Close. As Lucy walked around she saw other streets that were clearly named after different kinds of teeth – Wisdom Walk, Incisor Avenue, Gap Gardens and Wobbly Alley. The houses on Wobbly Alley looked a bit lopsided, Lucy thought.

'Goldie and Bonnie will give you a quick tour while I go and prepare the Wing Rooms for your arrival,' Queen Eldora told them.

'The *Wing* Rooms?' Lucy gasped.

The fairy queen nodded. 'That's where we'll fit you with your own set of fairy wings – and teach you how to use them. But first my fairies will show you everything else!'

Goldie and Bonnie led the children to a

staircase in the middle of the square. There were a few fairies flitting about here and there and some were standing in little groups, chatting to each other. All of them turned to stare as the children passed by. 'This is Upper Square,' Goldie explained, seemingly oblivious to the attention they were receiving. 'We have a full set of houses here and another full set in Lower Square, which is directly below us. Tooth-fairy Land is constructed just like a set of teeth,' she added proudly.

They walked down the twisty staircase and came out into another, almost identical square to the one they had just left.

'That's the Tooth Works,' Goldie said, pointing to a large tooth-house on their right. 'That's where our fairy dentists and their assistants make all the replacement teeth we leave under children's pillows.'

Goldie led them inside the Tooth Works, into a large room where about twenty fairies in short white coats were sitting at long tables using hammers and chisels and tiny fairy drills to turn various lumps of a hard white substance (which Bonnie explained was fairy-enamel) into replacement human teeth. The white coats were just like the kind human dentists wore, Lucy noticed, except that they had slits in the back for the wearer's wings to poke through.

'They're not being rude,' Bonnie explained quickly, as the fairy dentists noticed the children and turned round to stare at them just like the other fairies had done. 'Some of them have never seen a shrunken human before, that's all.'

Goldie and Bonnie offered to show them the Meeting Room next, which was

just a few houses along from the Tooth Works. 'We spend a lot of time there because Queen Eldora likes to hold at least one fairy meeting every day and we all take it in turns to attend,' Bonnie said as she led the way.

'I *hate* meetings,' Thomas said, pulling a face. 'Whenever we have them at school, they're always really boring. Dad says the ones he has to go to at work are really boring too, doesn't he, Lucy?'

'*Fairy* meetings aren't the least bit boring!' Bonnie told him. 'We all get to sit round the big meeting table and talk as much as we want to. Come and see!' She led them into a building that seemed to have just one huge room inside it – a room that contained the biggest oval table that Lucy had ever seen. There had to be about a hundred chairs around the table and at one end was a much higher chair, a bit like the ones Lucy had seen lifeguards sit on at the seaside. 'The Chair-fairy sits up there and keeps the air sprinkled with fairy dust the whole time,' Bonnie explained. 'Then we all start to talk at once and any good ideas that come out of the meeting react with the fairy dust and turn into gold sparks – which the fairy secretaries rush around trying to catch in their magic nets. Then Queen Eldora examines all the ideas in the nets, and the fairy who thought up the best one gets a gold star to stick on her toothbrush.'

'*I've* got six gold stars already,' Goldie put in. 'Bonnie's only got three but that's because she's a bit shy in meetings so she doesn't speak up as much.'

'Look,' Bonnie said, as they stepped outside again. She was pointing across the

square to a building that seemed to be  glowing more brightly than the others. 'That's the Goodness Factory. Now we're going to show you exactly what happens to children's teeth after we collect them!'

'You've heard the expression *"as good as gold"*, haven't you?' Goldie said. 'Well, that's where it comes from – because Goodness is golden in colour!'

They were inside the Goodness Factory now, and Lucy and Thomas were speechless as they stared at a massive gold container that was set into the floor and took up virtually the whole room. It was the size of a small swimming pool and it was filled with a gold-coloured sparkling dust.

'*That's* Goodness?' Lucy murmured in awe.

'Yes,' Goldie replied. 'We make it by combining children's teeth with fairy kisses – it's quite easy really. Watch!' She led them into another room where a human tooth – now the size of a large football in comparison to them – was sitting on a table.

Goldie and Bonnie carried the tooth back into the first room and then they flew up into the air with it so that they were holding the tooth over the pool of Goodness. Then Goldie kissed it. Immediately the tooth exploded into a mass of golden dust that sparkled as brightly as sunshine as it showered downwards.

'WOW!' Lucy and Thomas gasped.

'At least we've still got all *this* Goodness left,' Goldie said, 'but the way it works is this. For every tooth a fairy collects, she

100

gets a handful of Goodness dust to take  back to her own sector. The more children who give us their teeth in any particular sector, the more Goodness dust gets sprinkled about in the area where they live.'

'So if we don't stop Precious stealing all the teeth from *our* sector,' Bonnie continued, 'the Goodness levels *there* are going to go down really badly.'

'You mean the Goodness levels where *we* live?' Lucy asked, not liking the sound of that at all.

'Yes,' Goldie replied. 'We think Precious must actually be *living* somewhere in our sector, because no matter how quickly we respond when we find out that a tooth needs collecting, she *always* manages to get there before we do!'

'How do you know when a tooth needs collecting?' Thomas asked curiously.

'We see it on our pillow map,' Bonnie said.

'Your *pillow* map?'

Bonnie nodded. 'Each fairy sector has its own map and every time a tooth gets put under a pillow anywhere in that sector, the exact spot on the map lights up. Then we go off straight away to collect it. We all keep maps of our own sectors pinned up inside our houses and we check them every night.'

'Is that why Queen Eldora warned me not to let my teeth touch my pillow when I was showing them to her?' Lucy asked, remembering the fairy queen's reaction when she had tipped them out on to her bed.

'Yes. You see, we think Precious must've made her own pillow map – and that's how she knows when a tooth is being left for us.'

'It's very complicated being a tooth fairy,

isn't it?' Lucy said thoughtfully. 'What with all these maps and meetings and rules about everything?'

'You can say that again,' Bonnie and Goldie said, giggling. 'It's like we told you – flower fairies have *much* more fun!'

In the Wing Fitting Room, Queen Eldora was waiting for them along with two boy fairies who were dressed in dark-coloured, pinstriped suits.

'These are our fairy tailors,' Queen Eldora said. 'It's their job to measure you for your new wings.'

The fairy tailors each produced a measuring tape and started to take all sorts of strange measurements. Lucy stood as still as she could while she was measured from her belly button to her elbow, from

her nose to her fingertips, and from the tips of her ears to the centre of her back. Thomas, however, was getting more and more fidgety the longer he had to stand still.

Finally, when the measuring was finished, the children were led into a room that had a rail of fairy dresses on one side and a rail of smart suits on the other.

'We thought you might want to change out of your nightclothes,' Queen Eldora said. 'So please choose whatever you would most like to wear.'

'That's easy,' Thomas said, going over to the rail and picking the first pair of trousers and matching jacket that he came to. Thomas never spent much time fussing over clothes.

Neither did Lucy normally, but now she hovered by the dresses, unable to make up her mind. She never usually wore dresses at all but, if she was going to be a fairy for the night, she suddenly felt like she wanted to. In the end she chose a short turquoise dress that had sparkly sequins sewn all over it. When she stepped out of the fairy changing cubicle, Goldie and Bonnie beamed in delight and told her how pretty she looked.

'There's a pair of turquoise wings with silver stars on them that would look great with that dress,' Goldie told her, sounding excited. 'Let's go into the Wing Chamber and see if we can find them.'

The Wing Chamber turned out to be a huge, bright room with a high domed ceiling where spare pairs of fairy wings were flying around everywhere.

'We keep these here in case a fairy's own wings get damaged and they can't use them,' Bonnie explained. 'Or in case we get visitors like you!' As she spoke, one of the fairy tailors was using a long pole with a hook on the end of it to try and catch a pair of large silver wings for Thomas. 'Those are the turquoise ones up there – look!' Bonnie pointed them out, and the second fairy tailor appeared with another pole and began to chase after them.

Eventually both pairs of wings had been brought down from the ceiling. The fairy tailors measured both sets and declared they ought to fit the children perfectly.

It was a weird process having the wings fitted. Lucy watched while Thomas's were attached first. He had to have a special fairy ointment rubbed on to his back, then the wings were opened out and held against him. Lucy stared in amazement as tiny gold sparks appeared at the spot where the wings touched Thomas's body – and by the time the sparks had fizzled out, Thomas and the wings were united.

Next, Lucy underwent the same procedure, feeling a strange ticklish feeling on her back as the magic reaction took place. She stared at herself in the mirror afterwards, hardly able to believe that she had been transformed into a fairy – or at least a girl who looked exactly like a fairy.

'They feel weird.' Thomas kept putting his hands behind his back to touch the wings. 'I mean, I can feel them on my back, but when I try and touch them with my hands, it's like I'm just touching air!'

'False wings always feel a little strange until you get used to them,' Queen Eldora explained.

'Can we fly with them?' Lucy asked.

'Of course!'

'How?' Thomas asked.

'The best way to start is to *pretend* to be flying,' Queen Eldora advised them.

'How do you mean?' Thomas said.

'Do you mean we should pretend the way Izzy does when she's playing at being a fairy?' Lucy asked.

'Exactly!'

'But all Izzy does is run around on tiptoe

in those silly plastic wings and *tell* everyone she's flying,' Thomas pointed out.

'Yes, but she also *imagines* that she's flying,' Queen Eldora said, smiling. 'And the imagination is a very powerful thing – especially in Fairyland!'

Lucy closed her eyes and tried to imagine that she was a real fairy and she thought she felt her new wings flapping behind her just a little bit. She opened her eyes to glance across at her brother. Thomas never liked playing pretend games of any sort, and she was sure that he would never pretend to be a fairy.

But to Lucy's surprise, Thomas's wings were now starting to flap even more than hers. In fact they were flapping so much that he was now being lifted right off the ground.

'I'm imagining I'm Peter Pan!' Thomas

said, waving to her as he went whizzing up into the air.

'But Peter Pan wasn't a fairy,' Lucy shouted after him.

'It doesn't matter who he was, so long as he could fly,' Goldie told her.

'Come on, Lucy!' Thomas yelled down to her. 'Imagine you're Tinkerbell – that should do it!'

Lucy closed her eyes again and found that it was much easier to imagine herself flying now that she had seen Thomas doing it for real. Seconds later she was being lifted up off the ground too and then they had a wonderful time, practising flying backwards and forwards and upwards and downwards, and how to fly through narrow spaces and how to land without too much of a bump, until they felt like they'd been able to fly forever.

But finally Queen Eldora made the children come down to the ground again so that she could go over her plan with them.

'When you go back home, you will be your normal size again – apart from your wings. They will still be attached to you but they will remain fairy-sized. At six o'clock tomorrow morning, you must go out to

meet Precious in the garden as planned. Once you give her Lucy's teeth, she'll tell you where Izzy is and one of you must go and fetch Izzy straight away. But the other one can follow Precious.'

'So it doesn't have to be Lucy who follows Precious?' Thomas said quickly.

'I don't mind which of you it is – you can decide that between you.'

'But, Queen Eldora, you just said we'll be our normal size again,' Lucy pointed out, frowning. 'So how can we follow Precious without her seeing us?'

'Before you leave, I will give you a bag of fairy shrinking dust. All you have to do is sprinkle it over whichever one of you decides to follow Precious. It will work almost instantly.' She paused. 'Now, remember, I don't want you to try and catch Precious this time. All we need is for you to tell us where her hiding place is so that *we* can catch her!'

'What will you do to her when you find her?' Lucy wanted to know.

'We'll have to have a fairy meeting to decide that,' Queen Eldora answered. 'Now then, I want you to go back to bed and get some sleep before the morning, but remember to set your alarm clock for six o'clock, won't you?' As she spoke, she handed Lucy a little gold bag, which contained the shrinking dust the children were going to need the following morning. 'Here you are and *good luck*!'

It was almost as if the words '*good luck!*' were magical, because as soon as the fairy queen uttered them, Lucy found that her wings were lifting her

off the ground and carrying her upwards
again – and that Thomas was right behind
her.

'Close your eyes and imagine you're
home and you'll get there even quicker!'
Goldie called out after them.

So both children closed their eyes and,
the next thing they knew, they were back in
Lucy's bedroom, human-sized again, still
wearing their fairy clothes, which had
become human-sized along with them.
They still had their wings, but the children
could hardly feel them now, because they
had remained fairy-sized. They were both
so tired and so desperate to get some sleep
before they had to get up again in a few
hours' time that they fell straight into bed,
completely forgetting to set Lucy's alarm
clock.

9

At six o'clock the next morning, Lucy and Thomas were still fast asleep – but somebody else in the house wasn't. Grandpa had woken early and got up to use the bathroom. On his way back to bed he decided to have a look in the children's bedrooms to see if he could find his missing dentures. He was sure that Thomas had stolen them, and that they would therefore be hidden somewhere in Lucy's room.

He crept into the children's bedroom, limping slightly because his bad hip was

playing up, and once inside he looked around trying to spot likely hiding places for his teeth. It was difficult to see very well in the dim light that was coming in from the landing. He moved over to Lucy's chest of drawers, taking care not to disturb Thomas, who was on the camp bed in the middle of the floor. He opened the top drawer and started to rummage about among the socks, and although he didn't find his teeth, he did find a tiny key. He took it out and peered at it closely.

Right in front of him, on top of the chest of drawers, was Lucy's jewellery box, which he judged was just about large enough to hold his dentures if the children had removed them from their container. He had just fitted the key into the lock when a noise at the window made him turn.

Something gold and red was flying in

through the open window. He squinted to see better and as the object came closer he saw that it was a fairy in a gold dress and bright red boots.

'Well I never!' he exclaimed loudly – and his voice made Lucy and Thomas wake up with a start.

'Grandpa!' Lucy burst out, not seeing Precious straight away.

But her grandfather wasn't even looking in her direction. He was still staring at Precious, who was now hovering in the air above the jewellery box.

Lucy leaped clumsily out of bed as she spotted the fairy herself. 'Leave my teeth alone, Precious! You have to give Izzy back to us before you get them. Where is she? What have you done with her?'

'I *thought* you were going to meet me in the garden,' Precious replied curtly. 'But

since you didn't bother to show up, I thought I'd better come and find you.'

Lucy looked at her alarm clock and saw that it was already ten past six. 'Oh no!'

'What's all this about Izzy?' Grandpa asked.

Lucy saw that although he was talking to her, his gaze was still fixed firmly on Precious. 'Grandpa, can *you* see Precious too then?' she asked him.

'Of course I can! I may be short-sighted but I'm not blind!'

'But that means . . . that means you must believe in fairies,' Thomas said, rubbing his eyes as he got out of bed.

'That's right.'

'But . . . but you're a grown-up!' And a very crotchety old grown-up at that, Thomas felt like adding.

Grandpa laughed. 'Your grandmother

got me believing in fairies. She was always seeing them, and once or twice when we were outside in the garden together, I'd see one too.' He had turned to look at the children now, who were both still wearing their fairy clothes from the night before. 'In fact, they looked a bit like you do in those clothes – wherever did you get them?'

'This is all very interesting, I'm sure,' Precious interrupted impatiently, 'but I haven't got all day – and neither has Izzy. I'm presuming you still want her back?'

'Of course we want her back!' Lucy and Thomas exclaimed.

'What's *happened* to Izzy?' Grandpa asked again, looking worried.

'Precious has kidnapped her,' Thomas said.

'And she'll only give Izzy back if I give her all the baby teeth I've saved up,' Lucy

added, going over to open her jewellery box.

'*Kidnapped* her?' Grandpa looked amazed.

'That's right,' Precious answered smugly, 'and kidnapping *her* was a much nicer experience than kidnapping those nasty old fake teeth that were all stuck together, I can tell you! I can't think who'd want to put *those* in their mouth.'

'Are you referring to my dentures?' Grandpa demanded, scowling.

'She's the one who took them, Grandpa,' Thomas explained, as he quickly went over to the wardrobe to fetch them. 'She only brought them back last night. We were going to give them to you in the morning.'

Grandpa took his teeth from Thomas and gave Precious a toothless glare. 'I'll need to give these a good scrub under the tap before I put them back in, now that *you've* had your grubby little hands on them,' he told her.

'Oh, I didn't *touch* them!' Precious said, wrinkling up her nose as if she found that thought quite disgusting.

Grandpa glared at Precious even more as he took his dentures off to the bathroom with him.

After he'd gone, Lucy handed Precious her pouch of baby teeth and asked, 'So where's our sister?'

'I've tied her to the tree at the bottom of your garden. Don't worry – she's quite all right. We played together the whole time she was with me and we had lots of fun. She's back to her normal size again now so you can't miss her. The rope that she's tied with is magic – you won't be able to untie it, or cut it, until I'm safely away from here. That's in case you've got any more ideas about trying to catch me in a butterfly net.'

'It was a fishing net actually,' Thomas told her.

'A *fishing* net?' Precious looked horrified, clearly seeing herself as perhaps a little like a butterfly, but certainly nothing like a fish.

'Just hurry up and go, Precious,' Lucy said impatiently. 'The quicker you get away from here, the quicker we can untie Izzy.'

As Precious exited through the window and flew off to her right, Lucy bent down to pick up the little gold bag that Queen

Eldora had given her and which she had hidden under her bed. Inside was the shrinking dust. Lucy opened the bag and tipped out the gold dust on to her hand. 'Look out the window and see if you can still see her,' she hissed at Thomas as she lifted up her arm, ready to sprinkle the handful of dust over her head. 'We don't want to lose her.'

'Hey, *I* want to be the one who follows Precious,' Thomas protested, stepping towards Lucy instead of going over to the window.

'Queen Eldora gave the shrinking dust to *me*,' Lucy told him.

'No she didn't. She gave it to both of us!'

Grandpa came back into the room while the children were arguing. He looked like his normal self again now that he had his teeth in. 'What's going on?' he demanded.

'Precious has taken Lucy's teeth and I'm going to follow her,' Thomas said.

'*I* am, you mean,' Lucy snapped.

'Don't be stupid. If you try and follow Precious, you'll only get scared or lost or something, because you're a girl!'

'Want a bet?' And before Thomas could stop her, Lucy had released the dust all over herself.

As she stepped away from him, Lucy felt the same dizzy sensation as before, when she had been shrunk by Queen Eldora, and the same tingling all over her body. Just in time she remembered to close her eyes and when she opened them again, everything had changed. This time though she still recognized her room – apart from the fact that there were now two giants walking around in it.

Thomas was shouting down at her, 'It's

not fair! You always get *everything*!' And his voice was ten times louder now that she was fairy-sized.

Lucy forced herself to forget about everything else and to imagine that she was a real fairy. She soon felt her wings flapping behind her in response and almost immediately she was being lifted up off the ground and out through the window.

Grandpa was so shocked he had to sit down on Lucy's bed. 'Even your grandmother wouldn't believe this,' he mumbled as he stared at his miniature flying granddaughter.

As soon as she got outside, Lucy spotted Izzy tied to the tree in the garden just as Precious had described, but there was no time to go and speak to her. Since Precious had turned to her right after she had flown out of the window, Lucy did the same,

straining her eyes to catch sight of the fairy in the distance. All those teeth would be heavy to carry, Lucy thought, so hopefully they would slow Precious down.

After Lucy had flown over four gardens, she saw something gold straight ahead of her, shimmering in the early-morning sun, and as she got closer she saw that it was Precious, who had stopped on top of a fence to rest. Precious had put down the bag, which Lucy now saw was the size of a large sack if you were a fairy instead of a human.

Lucy slowed down, taking care not to be spotted. If Precious saw her too soon, the spell that was keeping Izzy tied to the tree might not be broken. Lucy decided to wait on a nearby tree branch, but, as she did so, a massive brown bird, the same size as Lucy, landed beside her, making a deafening chirping noise in her ear. The bird was holding a huge, pink, wriggly earthworm in its beak. As the end of the giant worm squirmed towards her, Lucy screamed and toppled right off the branch. Luckily her wings immediately started to flap so she didn't fall far, and since Precious had already lifted up the sack of teeth and was flying on with it, Lucy hurriedly followed.

She stayed behind Precious as they flew over four more gardens, before the fairy turned to her right and flew upwards

towards the roof of a house, which Lucy realized must be situated in the same street as her own. The house had bare windows with no curtains and Lucy saw that it had no furniture inside it. One of the houses further down their road had been empty for a while – she passed it every day on her way to school – and she guessed that this was probably it. She watched Precious fly right up to the overhanging part of the roof and disappear.

Lucy couldn't understand where Precious had gone at first. Then, as she flew closer herself, she saw that up in the eaves of the house there was a gap that was just large enough for a small bird – or a fairy – to pass through. She flew through it and found that she was in a massive dark space, which she guessed must be the house's loft.

A light was coming from the far side of the space and, as Lucy flew towards it, she saw that she was approaching what seemed to be a small house *inside* the loft. For a moment she was confused, until she realized that what she was looking at was a doll's house.

Lucy cautiously peered in through one of the doll's house windows and saw that there were fairy lights strung up inside.

Suddenly the front door was flung open and Precious appeared in the entrance,

130

looking cross. 'I *thought* someone was following me. I couldn't smell a fairy so I thought it must be a bird. I might have known it was you!'

'Precious, please don't be angry,' Lucy said, feeling a bit frightened now that she had been caught.

'I suppose Queen Eldora gave you some shrinking dust so you could follow me, did she? Well, I'm not giving your teeth back if that's why you're here!'

'Can't we just talk about this?' Lucy said nervously, trying to buy herself some time.

'Why should I talk to you? You're only here to spy on me!' But despite her sharp

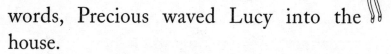

words, Precious waved Lucy into the house.

Lucy found herself in a little hall that had old-fashioned stripy wallpaper and a square of faded red carpet on the floor. Pinned up on one wall she saw a large, hand-drawn map of her own street and all the other streets in the surrounding neighbourhood. 'Is that a *pillow* map?' she asked, staring at it.

Precious nodded. 'I made it myself as soon as I got here. It's good, isn't it?'

'But I don't see any pillows on it,' Lucy said, peering at the map more closely.

'That's because the pillows are invisible! They only light up when someone leaves out a tooth!'

'Precious, the other fairies are really cross with you for stealing all the teeth,' Lucy said, turning to face her now.

133

'It's all right for *them*,' Precious said, scowling. '*They're* not stuck here with no way of getting back home again, are they?'

She led Lucy through a flimsy-looking door into the living room, which was full of weird-looking furniture. There was a fake fireplace that had coals and flames painted on to it, a pink sofa made of hard plastic that looked really uncomfortable to sit on, and a plastic standard lamp that was clearly fake too.

'How did you find this place?' Lucy asked.

'I was flying about looking for somewhere warm to sleep and I found this loft. I couldn't believe it when I found the doll's house too. I guess it must have got left behind when the owners moved out.'

'The fairy lights are really pretty!'

'I know. The people next door keep their

134

Christmas decorations up in *their* loft and I snuck in there one day and borrowed them. I've had to use fairy magic instead of electricity though!' Precious seemed to be relaxing a bit now. 'I'll give you a tour of the rest of the place, if you like,' she added. 'You're my first ever visitor – even if you are a spy!'

'Precious, I can see how you might want to borrow things that you really need, like fairy lights,' Lucy began carefully, as Precious led her back into the hall and up an alarmingly wobbly staircase, 'but I still don't see how you can *need* all the teeth you keep taking.'

'Oh, but I *do* need them!' Precious said. They were entering a little bedroom that had a wooden bed, a pink plastic wardrobe (which really opened) and some pink curtains that looked like they had gone a

bit mouldy. Precious had made a mattress for the bed out of leaves and a white cotton handkerchief, and she sat down on it now and looked up at Lucy.

'I don't understand,' Lucy said, frowning. '*Why* do you need them?'

'I need them for the same reason the other tooth fairies need them,' Precious told her. 'To make Goodness!'

Lucy stared at her, still not getting it. 'But *why*?' she asked. 'I mean why do you need to make Goodness separately from the other tooth fairies?'

'I'm making it to use on *myself*, of course,' Precious said. 'Everyone thinks I'm happy being bad, but I'm not. If you're bad, nobody likes you and you get left out of things – you even get left out of Fairyland. So I'm going to use the Goodness dust to turn myself into a *good* fairy!'

Lucy gaped at Precious, hardly able to believe what she was hearing.

'You can come and see if you like,' Precious offered, jumping up and leading the way across the landing into the bathroom, where the blue sack containing Lucy's teeth was propped up against the bath.

The bath itself was filled almost to the top with the same golden dust Lucy had seen before in the Goodness Factory, and Lucy stood and stared at it in amazement.

'When I've turned all *your* teeth into Goodness too, I reckon I'll have enough,' Precious said.

'Enough for *what?*' Lucy asked.

'Enough to make me good enough to pass through the Goodness curtain, of course!' Precious was starting to sound excited. 'Then I'll be able to go home to Fairyland!'

Lucy didn't know what to say. She found herself suddenly feeling quite sorry for Precious – and she wanted to help her get back to Fairyland again too. But she wasn't sure that the way Precious was planning to do it was the answer.

'You can stay and watch if you want,' Precious told her. 'There isn't time for you to go and fetch the other fairies now in any case.'

Before Lucy had time to reply, Precious removed the first tooth from the sack and flew up to hold it out over the bath. Then she leaned forward and kissed it – just like Goldie had done to the tooth in the Goodness Factory – and suddenly the tooth exploded into a cloud of golden dust.

The whole bathroom lit up as the Goodness dust showered down to join the rest already in the bath.

Precious took out the remaining five teeth one by one and repeated the action five times. Then, when all the teeth had been changed into Goodness, Precious asked Lucy to wait outside while she took her Goodness bath.

'You mean you're going to take a bath in *that*?' Lucy exclaimed.

'Of course. How else am I going to become a good fairy?'

'But are you sure it's *safe*?'

'How can Goodness *not* be safe?' Precious said. 'Though I might be *so* good when I come out that you won't recognize me!'

So Lucy went back into the bedroom to wait and, as she sat down on the bed, she started to feel a bit light-headed. At first she thought it was just all the excitement, but then she felt her arms and legs begin to tingle.

It was then that she remembered the shrinking spell. Goldie had told her that shrinking spells never lasted long if you were outside Fairyland. Her head was getting dizzier and as she felt the familiar tingling sensation spread over her body, she knew that she had to get out of the doll's house straight away.

Just in time, Lucy remembered her fairy wings. She dragged herself over to the window and flew out of it, making sure she headed straight for the ground. She landed just in time. One second she was fairy-sized and the next she was back to her full size again – sitting on the floor of the loft.

She stayed where she was, feeling her heart racing. She felt dizzy and a little bit sick. Everything looked completely different now. In front of her was the doll's house – looking toy-sized in comparison to before.

Suddenly Precious emerged from the front door and Lucy immediately saw that she looked different too – and not just because she seemed so much smaller. Her clothes, her skin and her shiny dark hair were all sparkling so brightly that just looking at her made Lucy blink.

'It worked!' Precious exclaimed. 'I'm covered in Goodness now. That silly Goodness curtain will *have* to let me through!'

'My shrinking spell's worn off,' Lucy said when it didn't seem as if Precious was going to mention it.

'You don't say,' Precious joked. 'Well, that's what happens, I'm afraid. Shrinking spells always wear off in the most inconvenient places! That's why I didn't even bring Izzy here. I'd used up my last bit of shrinking dust on her, so I knew I couldn't shrink her again when the spell wore off. I didn't want her to get trapped up here, you see.'

'Trapped?' Lucy looked around her in alarm. 'But there must be some way out.'

'There isn't. You can't get down into the house from up here.'

'But there must be some sort of door,' Lucy said, starting to feel anxious.

'There is, but it's been locked from the landing side.'

'Well, can't *you* get inside the house and unlock it?' Lucy asked her.

'I haven't got time,' Precious said. 'I have to get back to the Golden pillowcase before all this Goodness wears off.' She started to fly towards the fairy-sized hole that led

outside. 'You'll be all right. Once I'm back in Fairyland I'll tell Queen Eldora where you are. Then she'll send someone to let you out.'

'But that might take ages,' Lucy protested. 'You can't leave me here all on my own!'

'You'll be OK,' Precious said again. 'I won't forget about you. Don't worry.'

'Precious, please,' Lucy pleaded, hearing her voice begin to tremble. 'I'm frightened.'

Precious paused for a moment, frowning. Then she seemed to shake off any doubt about it as she snapped, 'You should have thought about that when you volunteered to come and spy on me! You weren't frightened *then*, were you?'

'Well, I am now,' Lucy said, fighting back tears.

But Precious had already disappeared through the hole in the roof.

11

Lucy desperately started to search for the door that led down into the main part of the house. She soon found it but, just as Precious had said, there seemed to be no way of opening it from her side. She tried to push the door downwards, then she tried pulling it upwards, but it wouldn't budge either way. Precious must be right about it being locked.

Lucy felt her mouth go dry. What was she going to do?

It was a horrible feeling being trapped,

and even though Precious had promised to send someone to help her when she reached Fairyland, Lucy didn't trust her to remember – at least, not straight away. Lucy might be stuck there for several hours, or even for the whole day. What would her parents think when they found out she was missing? Grandpa, Thomas and Izzy would all be worried too.

Lucy sat down in the middle of the loft, hugging her knees. Then, to make things even worse, the lights in the doll's house suddenly went out. She was in total darkness now. And, even though Lucy wasn't a child who cried easily, she felt a big tear roll down her cheek as she tried to stop trembling.

She thought about what Thomas would say – that she was scared because she was a

girl. She knew that wasn't true – girls were just as brave as boys – but even so she wished that Thomas was with her now. Maybe if she hadn't been so quick to use up all the shrinking dust on herself, they might have been able to share it between them. Then they could have followed Precious together while Grandpa went to rescue Izzy.

Lucy felt more and more guilty as she sat in the dark thinking about how she had brought all of this on herself. Even if there *hadn't* been enough shrinking dust for both her and Thomas, Lucy thought now, the fair thing would have been to flip a coin to decide who got to use it. She couldn't help wondering what Thomas would think when she didn't return home as planned. Maybe he wouldn't be worried about her at all. Maybe he would just feel pleased that she was gone. She felt even more alone as she thought that.

Suddenly she felt a draught at her back and she turned to see Precious hovering in the air behind her.

'Precious!' Lucy gasped. 'You came back!'

'I'd forgotten the lights would go out after I left,' Precious said, sounding apologetic. She snapped her fingers and the lights in the doll's house instantly came on again.

'Oh, Precious, thank you.' Lucy felt like crying with relief now.

'Yes . . . well . . . for some reason as soon as I flew away I started to feel guilty about leaving you,' Precious said, frowning, 'which is very strange since I don't usually feel guilty about *anything*. It wasn't a nice feeling at all. Anyway, I've decided I'd better get you out of here after all.'

'How?' Lucy asked, as Precious started to fly away from her again.

'I'll go down the chimney into the house and then I'll find the door to the loft and see how they've locked it. We'll have to do this very quickly though, before my Goodness dust wears off.' She had flown outside again before she'd even finished talking.

It wasn't long before Lucy heard Precious's high-pitched voice on the other side of the loft door. 'A removal van was pulling up outside as I flew down the chimney,' the fairy shouted out to her. 'I think the new owners must be arriving.'

'Well, hurry up then!' Lucy burst out, starting to panic again. 'What's the lock like? Can you undo it?'

'It's just a bolt,' Precious called back, 'but it's a bit stiff . . .' There was a long silence,

punctuated by little grunting noises as Precious tugged at it. 'All right, you can push the door now!'

The door itself was a bit stiff too at first, but Lucy soon managed to budge it and it swung open so suddenly that she only just stopped herself from falling through the hole.

'Your fairy wings won't support you now you're human-sized,' Precious told her, 'so you'll have to jump down.'

'It's too far to jump,' Lucy said. 'Isn't there a ladder we can borrow from somewhere?'

'There isn't time!'

'Well, I can't just jump!' Lucy protested. 'I'll hurt myself!'

Precious frowned as if she was thinking very carefully about something. 'I *could* use up the rest of my Goodness dust on you, I suppose,' she finally muttered. She quickly explained to Lucy what she meant. 'Once, when Goldie and Bonnie were in a children's playground sprinkling the air with Goodness dust, a little girl lost her hold on the climbing frame. They could see she was going to fall so they threw the rest of their Goodness dust on the ground where they thought she'd land – and she ended up having such a good landing that she wasn't hurt at all. I suppose I *could* try the same thing with you.' Precious reached inside the pockets of her dress and brought out two handfuls of golden dust.

'I thought you used up all your Goodness dust in your bath,' Lucy said in surprise.

'I kept a little bit back in case I needed a top-up when I got to the Goodness curtain,' Precious explained, as she

sprinkled the dust on to the floor directly under the loft entrance. 'Now *jump!*'

Lucy stared down at the sparkling carpet and jumped – landing on the floor with a thump that was ten times softer than she'd expected it to be.

'A very good landing!' Precious said approvingly. 'Now, let's go.'

They were just about to go down the stairs when the front door opened and voices sounded in the hall.

'Hide!' Precious hissed, pointing to one of the empty bedrooms. 'I'll go down and distract them. When I give the signal, you run downstairs and escape through the front door and I'll follow you and meet you back at your house.'

'*What* signal?' Lucy whispered, but Precious had already disappeared.

Two minutes later, Lucy heard a loud

crash coming from downstairs and she guessed that the signal had been given. The two adults who had been standing in the hallway headed off in the direction of the noise, which had come from the back of the house. Lucy knew that this was her chance to escape out the front. She tiptoed down the stairs, across the hall and out through the open door.

There was a large removal van outside and a car parked in the driveway, which Lucy guessed must belong to the new owners of the house. The removal men, who were starting to unload their van, stared at her as she ran past and one of them grunted, 'Where did *she* come from?' But they didn't try to stop her.

Lucy ran up the road towards her own house without looking back and when she got there she hurried round to the back

door where she hoped there would be someone to let her in.

She knocked on the door and it was opened immediately by Thomas.

'You've been ages!' he exclaimed. 'We were getting really worried about you! We've had to make Mum and Dad breakfast in bed to make sure they didn't get up and find out you'd gone.'

Izzy was in the kitchen too and Lucy was so relieved to see her back to her normal size again that she rushed over to give her little sister a hug. 'We got such

a fright when Precious kidnapped you, Izzy! Are you OK now?'

'Oh yes!' Izzy exclaimed. 'I've had a lovely time! Precious let me try on her red boots and play with her magic toothbrush and everything! You look really pretty in that dress, Lucy!'

'Where's Grandpa?' Lucy asked. 'He hasn't said anything to Mum and Dad about the fairies, has he?'

'Don't worry – he's being really cool about everything,' Thomas answered. 'He's upstairs getting dressed now but he'll be down in a minute. So did you find out where Precious is hiding?'

'Yes, but Thomas, listen . . . I'm really sorry for taking all the shrinking dust for myself like that. It was really selfish and you're right – it wasn't fair.'

Thomas looked taken aback, and Lucy

realized that he wasn't used to being on the receiving end of an apology. Usually it was Thomas who was being made to say sorry to her or Izzy for something bad that *he'd* done.

'It wasn't fair,' he agreed, 'but I'd probably have done the same if *I'd* got to the dust first.' He paused. 'So come on . . . tell me what happened . . . Did you find Precious?'

'Yes, but I think maybe we were wrong about her,' Lucy said. 'I don't think she *is* all that bad – not really.'

'I *like* Precious,' Izzy said firmly. 'I know it was naughty of her to steal Grandpa's teeth and to catch me in our net, but we *did* try to catch her first! And she looked after me really well the whole time I was with her.'

'Precious helped *me* in the end too,' Lucy

said, quickly explaining to them what had happened when she'd got trapped inside the loft.

'So where is she then?' Thomas asked.

'I'm not sure,' Lucy said. 'I thought she'd be here by now. I think I'd better go back and look for her.'

'I'll come with you,' said Izzy.

'*Precious!*' Lucy exclaimed as soon as they stepped outside. The fairy was waiting for them out in the garden and she wasn't looking very happy. 'We were just coming to find you! Are you all right?'

'Do I *look* like I'm all right?' Precious grunted.

'You look just the same to me,' Thomas said as he joined them.

'Exactly!' Precious said grumpily.

That's when Lucy realized what the problem was. 'You aren't sparkling any

more, are you?' she said. 'Does that mean all your Goodness dust has worn off?'

Precious nodded glumly. 'I spent so long helping you escape that it's all gone. I even used up my *extra* dust on you!'

'Oh, Precious, I'm really sorry,' Lucy said softly.

'Now I won't be able to get through the Goodness curtain after all,' Precious said in a shaky voice.

'How does the Goodness curtain work exactly?' Izzy asked, since she was the only one who hadn't seen it in action.

Lucy quickly explained it to her. 'So Precious thought that if she covered herself in Goodness dust, the curtain might let her through,' she finished. 'But she took so long helping me that now she can't try it out.'

'I don't understand,' Izzy said, frowning.

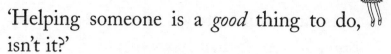

'Helping someone is a *good* thing to do, isn't it?'

'Yes, but . . .' Lucy broke off as she began to see what Izzy was getting at. She stopped to think something through for a moment, before turning to face Precious. 'Precious, I'm pretty sure Queen Eldora said that the Goodness curtain works by testing how good you are on the *inside*. And if that's the case it's still worth you trying to get through because your *inner* Goodness levels must have gone up loads since you came back to help me.'

'Do you really think so?' Precious looked surprised. 'I didn't mean to do anything good – it just sort of happened.'

'Well, that still must've changed your Goodness levels, mustn't it?'

'I suppose so,' Precious agreed. 'But do

you really think they could have gone up *enough*?'

'There's only one way to find out,' Lucy said. 'Come on!' Feeling hopeful, she led the way across the lawn towards the fence that separated their garden from their neighbours'. The golden pillowcase was still hanging on their neighbours' washing line.

Precious hovered just above the fence, eyeing the pillowcase nervously.

'Go on then!' Thomas urged her. 'What are you waiting for?'

'What if it doesn't work?' Precious mumbled.

'You've got nothing to lose by *trying*, have you?' Lucy reminded her gently.

So with the three children watching – Thomas had to lift Izzy up so that she could see over the fence too – Precious flew off towards the pillowcase.

'Good luck!' the children all shouted together.

And the last glimpse they had of Precious was of her red shiny boots as she disappeared from view.

12

'If she doesn't come back, we'll know the Goodness curtain has let her through,' Lucy said.

As the children waited, Thomas continued to hold Izzy even though she was really too heavy for him, and Lucy thought that this was the closest she'd ever seen the two of them.

'You know, we're much luckier than fairies,' Thomas said suddenly, looking thoughtful.

'How do you mean?' Lucy asked.

'Well, it doesn't matter how good or bad we are, our parents would love us just the same, wouldn't they? I mean, they'd never say we weren't allowed to come home again.'

Lucy hadn't thought about that before. 'You're right,' she agreed. 'Imagine if *we* had to pass through a Goodness curtain every time *we* wanted to go home!'

'I'd hardly ever be allowed in,' Thomas said, grinning.

'That would be horrible,' Izzy gasped.

'Precious has made it, I think,' Lucy said.

Thomas nodded, setting Izzy down on the ground. 'Come on. Let's go back inside and tell Grandpa.'

Grandpa was entering the kitchen as they walked in through the back door and he looked relieved when he saw Lucy. 'We were wondering where you'd got to,' he said to her. 'Are you all right?'

She nodded. 'Thanks for helping us, Grandpa.'

'No problem at all. I told your parents I found my dentures under my pillow during the night. I said I'd put them there myself and totally forgotten about them. Now they think I'm losing my memory, but still . . . They're feeling quite guilty about blaming you children for taking them so I think you might be in for a treat or two today. Now, Lucy . . . Tell me what's been happening with those fairies . . .'

Lucy told him everything, and when her dad came downstairs five minutes later, the three children and their grandfather were sitting round the kitchen table chatting and giggling together.

'What's going on?' Dad asked, hardly able to believe what he was seeing – his father and his children never got on as well as this.

'We're having a private conversation,' Grandpa said, tapping the side of his nose, 'about fairies.'

All three children gasped out loud, but they soon saw that it didn't matter that Grandpa had told the truth.

'Fairies, eh?' Dad said, sounding amused.

'*Tooth* fairies actually,' Grandpa added.

'Well, as long as you kids aren't planning on asking the Tooth Fairy to increase the money she gives you for your teeth, you can talk about her all you like,' Dad said jokily.

'He really doesn't believe in fairies, does he?' Thomas said as the doorbell rang and their father went to answer it.

'No, and I'll tell you why.' Grandpa had a twinkle in his eye. 'It's because he's middle-aged. Children and old folk are the ones who believe in fairies. Middle-aged people hardly ever do.'

'Why don't they?' Izzy asked.

Grandpa shrugged. 'Maybe it's because they're too busy worrying about other things – like their children and their old folk!'

'Dad says he's worried about his middle-age spread too,' Lucy added, which made Grandpa laugh.

'*I'm* still going to believe in fairies when *I'm* middle-aged,' Thomas said firmly.

Lucy and Izzy both agreed that they would too.

Just then the children's father came back into the room holding a tiny white envelope in his hand. 'There was no one

there when I opened the door,' he said, sounding puzzled. 'But this had been posted through the letter box. There's no writing on it and there's nothing inside except a blank card.'

'Let me see,' Lucy said. As Dad handed her the envelope she saw the sparkly gold writing on the front straight away – *To Lucy, Thomas and Izzy.*

She quickly opened it. There were two things inside the envelope – a little card (which also had sparkly writing on it) and a loose gold star.

Lucy shook the gold star out on to the table and picked up the card to read it:

Dear Lucy, Thomas and Izzy,
You are invited to attend our fairy meeting tonight, where Queen Eldora has something very important she wishes to discuss with you. Afterwards there will be a party where you will be the guests of honour. Please be waiting for us by the golden pillowcase at midnight tonight.

Love from,
The Tooth Fairies

PS This writing will only be visible to those who believe in fairies.
PPS Please reply with the gold star if you can come.

At the bottom of the invitation were the letters *RSVP*, followed by a star-shaped

outline, where you were obviously meant to stick the gold star if your answer to the invitation was yes.

Lucy handed the invitation to Thomas and Izzy to read, and Grandpa leaned over to look at it too. Mum came into the room while this was happening and Dad told her, 'I think they're playing some sort of pretend game.'

The children were so excited that they quickly left the grown-ups and rushed upstairs.

'But how will we get our reply back to them?' Izzy asked as they carefully stuck the little gold star on to the bottom of the card.

Before she had even finished speaking, the card had floated out of Lucy's hand. The envelope that they had left on Lucy's bed was lifting itself up into the air to

169

join it. The card slipped itself inside the envelope and the children ran to the window to watch as the letter flew outside and disappeared in the direction of the golden pillowcase.

For the rest of the day the children could think about nothing except the fairy party. Izzy was especially excited since she had never been to Fairyland before, and she kept asking Lucy and Thomas lots of questions about what it was like there.

'It's not *just* a party,' Thomas reminded his sisters, as they all gathered in Lucy's room that afternoon. 'We've got to go to the fairy meeting too, remember.'

'Maybe we'd better take two outfits,' Izzy suggested. 'One for the meeting and one for the party.'

'Knowing Queen Eldora, her meeting

might go on for so long that we don't even get to the party,' Thomas said.

'Don't be silly,' Lucy said quickly, seeing how worried Izzy was looking. 'There *will* be a party, Izzy. It's just that we might have to sit through quite a long meeting first.'

'Maybe we could sleep through the meeting,' Thomas joked. 'I fell asleep once in a meeting we had at school and it made it pass much quicker!'

'Goldie and Bonnie said that *fairy* meetings are fun,' Lucy reminded him. 'But we might still feel sleepy, so I reckon we should go to bed really early tonight and try and get some rest before we go to Fairyland. I can set my alarm clock to wake us up before midnight. What do you think?'

'Your alarm clock didn't wake us up this morning, did it?' Thomas pointed out.

'Only because I forgot to set it,' Lucy said. 'But to be extra sure, we could ask Grandpa to come and check we're awake at midnight as well. He's always getting up in the night to use the bathroom anyway, so I don't think he'd mind.'

'Grandpa's gone all grumpy again,' Izzy pointed out. 'He might not want to help us.'

Lucy and Thomas looked at Izzy. It was true that ever since the fairy invitation had arrived, Grandpa had been keeping himself to himself, just like he usually did. At lunchtime he had hardly eaten a thing and he'd gone up to his room straight away afterwards, saying that he needed to rest.

'Maybe his bad hip is playing him up,' Lucy said. 'Why don't we go and see him?'

So they went and knocked on Grandpa's door.

'Come in,' Grandpa grunted, so quietly that they only just heard him.

They went inside and found him sitting in the armchair by the window looking fed up.

'Grandpa, is something wrong?' Lucy asked immediately.

Grandpa turned his face away from her and didn't reply.

'Is your hip hurting you?' Izzy asked, taking a step towards him.

'My hip's always hurting me,' Grandpa grunted. 'Nothing new there.'

The children didn't know what else to say. They looked at each other and shrugged, but just as they were beginning to leave, Grandpa suddenly added, 'Just because I've got a bad hip, it doesn't mean I can't still enjoy a good party.'

Lucy frowned, not really following him.

'*If* I was to be invited to one, that is,' Grandpa said sharply.

Then Lucy thought she understood what the problem was. 'Grandpa, are you upset because the tooth fairies didn't invite you to their party?'

'Of course I'm upset!' Grandpa snapped. '*I* believed in fairies long before you three did and this is how they thank me!'

'I'm sure they didn't mean to leave you out, Grandpa,' Thomas said quickly. 'I expect they just didn't realize you'd want to come with us, that's all.'

'Well, they *should* realize! Insensitive little creatures! I really don't know why your grandmother bothered with them so much!'

'Grandpa, why don't you just come with us to the party anyway?' Lucy said. 'The fairies will be glad to see you, I'm sure.

They probably just didn't think of inviting you because you're a grown-up.'

'Do you think so?' Grandpa asked, sniffing.

'Of course! Anyway, *we* want you to come with us, don't we?' she added, looking at the others.

'Yes, Grandpa, we do,' Izzy and Thomas both said together.

'Well, if you really think I should come . . .' Grandpa was beginning to look a bit cheerier. 'I shall have to look out something to wear. The trouble is, I haven't brought any smart clothes with me.'

'*I* think you should wear these,' Izzy said, pointing to their grandfather's red-and-green-striped pyjamas, which were neatly folded up on top of the bed. 'I think they're *much* nicer than the clothes you wear during the day.'

Grandpa laughed. 'I might just do that Izzy,' he said. 'After all, it's nice to wear bright clothes to a party, isn't it?'

'It's not *just* a party,' Thomas reminded them all. 'We have to go to a fairy meeting first.'

'Oh yes, the fairy *meeting* . . .' Grandpa frowned because as a rule he didn't tend to like meetings very much either. 'I wonder what *that's* going to be about.'

'Queen Eldora is always having meetings,' Lucy replied. 'It probably won't be about anything in particular.'

But as it happened, Lucy was wrong . . .

Lucy remembered the Meeting Room from her earlier trip to Fairyland, when Goldie and Bonnie had been showing her and Thomas around. But when they got there shortly after midnight she hardly recognized it.

The noise was deafening because the room was now filled with at least a hundred chattering fairies who were sitting round the table waiting for them. There didn't seem to be a Chair-fairy today, but on a high throne at the end of the table Queen

Eldora was presiding. She had sent Goldie and Bonnie to fetch the children and now she smiled in greeting as they entered the room. She looked surprised to see Grandpa, whom the two fairies had readily agreed to shrink down and bring through the golden pillowcase to Fairyland along with the children.

Izzy was the most excited to be there. She had beamed with delight as they travelled in the fairy lift, and in the town square she had gasped out loud at the fairy houses. She had dressed in her own fairy costume for the visit, which had magically shrunk down in size when she did, so that apart from the fact that she didn't have wings, she looked just like a real fairy. Lucy and Thomas still had their wings from the last time they had been there and they were wearing their fairy

clothes again too. And Grandpa looked very cheery in his red-and-green-striped pyjamas.

'Come and sit beside me!' a familiar voice called to them.

They looked across to see Precious sitting at the table. She had saved seats for the three children on either side of her and now one of the other fairies moved along to make room for Grandpa too.

As they all sat down, Queen Eldora clapped her hands for silence. 'Welcome to our fairy meeting!' she announced. 'And an especially warm welcome to our guests – Lucy, Thomas, Izzy and . . .' She broke off, looking politely at Grandpa, whom she had never met before.

'This is our grandfather,' Thomas said. 'He believes in fairies too.'

'We thought it would be all right to

bring him,' Goldie and Bonnie said. 'He was quite easy to shrink.'

'I'm very pleased to meet you,' Queen Eldora told Grandpa. 'And I now have even more pleasure in declaring this meeting – our first ever to include humans as well as fairies – officially open!' She waved her toothbrush in the air, which the children

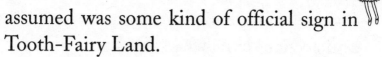

assumed was some kind of official sign in Tooth-Fairy Land.

'As you all know, this is a very special day,' Queen Eldora began, smiling as she looked round the table at all her fairies. 'I'm pleased to announce that Precious has passed the test of the Goodness curtain at last, and although she is going to have to work very hard at being a good fairy from now on, at least she is back among us again.'

A cheer went up at the table and Precious beamed with pleasure.

'And now we can all get on with doing what we do best – collecting children's teeth and making Goodness out of them!' the fairy queen declared.

Another cheer went up.

'However, Precious would not be back with us,' Queen Eldora continued, 'if it

wasn't for the help we've had from the human children who are here with us tonight — and, in particular, Lucy. Lucy, please stand up so we may all applaud you.'

Lucy remained seated, blushing with the sudden attention, and she only stood when Thomas and Precious pushed her to her feet. Queen Eldora was flourishing her golden toothbrush in the air again and calling out for everyone to listen carefully. 'The reason I have called this meeting is to ask each of these children what they would like as a thank-you gift from us. Secretary fairies, get ready to note down their wishes!'

Three fairies in purple dresses came flying into the middle of the table, where they hovered with notepads and sparkly pens in their hands.

'You may have one wish each,' Queen

Eldora told the children, 'so choose carefully.'

Everyone turned to look at Lucy, who quickly sat down again, muttering, 'I'm not sure I know what to ask for.'

'Ask for a year's supply of sweets,' Thomas whispered in her ear.

Lucy ignored him and asked if she could have some more time to think about it.

Queen Eldora nodded and turned to Izzy, who was looking very excited. 'Do you know what wish *you* would like granted, Izzy?'

'I'd like some fairy wings, please, like the ones you gave Lucy and Thomas,' Izzy said.

The fairy secretaries wrote down Izzy's request and Queen Eldora waved her toothbrush in the air and pronounced it done.

'Goldie and Bonnie will take you to the Wing Rooms directly after the meeting,' she told Izzy. She paused for a moment to look at Grandpa, who seemed a bit agitated about something. 'I sense that the children's grandfather would also like to borrow some fairy wings,' she said. 'Am I right?'

Grandpa instantly nodded. 'If it wouldn't be too much trouble.'

'Of course not. You can go to the Wing Rooms after the meeting along with Izzy. But this time you must all give back your wings before you leave Fairyland.'

'Excuse me, Queen Eldora,' Grandpa said before the fairy queen's attention could move away from him. 'There's just one other thing I'd like to ask you, if I may.'

'Of course.'

'I haven't seen a fairy in my garden for a very long time and I was wondering if you

knew why – and what I could do to make them come back again?'

'I assume you are talking of flower fairies?' the fairy queen said.

'Well, I assume so, yes,' Grandpa agreed, not liking to say that until recently he had thought that there was only one type of fairy.

'And how long is it exactly since you saw a fairy in your garden?'

'Not since my wife died and that was nearly eight years ago.'

'And when your wife was alive, did she do anything to encourage these fairies to visit you?' Queen Eldora asked.

Grandpa was about to shake his head, when he remembered something. 'Now I come to think of it, they did always seem to visit us whenever she'd just been baking.'

'What did she bake?'

'Well . . . all kinds of things really. Jam tarts sometimes. Crispy cakes. Scones. That sort of thing. She and I both had a bit of a sweet tooth, you see.'

'I *do* see,' Queen Eldora said, sighing. 'And were the crispy cakes *chocolate* ones?'

Grandpa nodded. 'Yes.'

Queen Eldora was looking around at her fairies now. 'Shall we tell the children's grandfather how he can get to see more flower fairies?' she asked them.

Immediately the fairies all started to grin as they shouted out the same word at once: 'CHOCOLATE!'

'Flower fairies don't worry in the slightest about their teeth, so they don't mind how much chocolate they eat,' Queen Eldora told Grandpa. 'The more the better, as far as they're concerned. So leaving out

chocolate is an excellent way to get them to visit you.'

'I'll leave some out on my bird table as soon as I get home,' Grandpa said, looking pleased. 'Chocolate, eh? I'd never have thought of that.'

A lot of the fairies were talking excitedly about chocolate now and Queen Eldora had to wave her toothbrush to get everyone's attention again.

She turned to Thomas, who had been sitting very quietly through all of this. 'Thomas, have *you* decided what wish you would like us to grant you?' she asked him.

Lucy fully expected her brother to ask for a year's supply of sweets, or even *two* years' supply, but instead he looked quite nervous as he stammered out his request. 'There *is* something I wondered if you

could do for me,' he said. 'You see, sometimes . . . when I come to stay at my dad's house . . . it would be really nice . . . really special . . . if I could get to spend some time on my own with him.'

Lucy, Izzy and Grandpa all looked at him in surprise.

'Have you not *asked* your father for this?' Queen Eldora was clearly also surprised by Thomas's request.

'Sort of. One time he told me he was going fishing and I asked if I could go with him because I thought it was just going to be the two of us. But then everyone else wanted to come too and he seemed to like that idea better. So I didn't like to ask him again after that.'

'But, Thomas,' Lucy said, sounding dismayed, '*I* was the one who asked Dad if we could all go fishing. I never knew you

wanted time on your own with him. Why didn't you say something?'

Thomas shrugged. 'I didn't like to. I mean, how do I know that Dad *wants* to spend time just with me? It's not like *he's* suggested it, is it?'

'Well, he should have,' Grandpa said briskly. 'I'll have a word with him if you like, Thomas. You don't need to use up your fairy wish on this.'

'I *want* this as my fairy wish,' Thomas said. 'That way I know it will really happen.'

The fairy secretaries were writing furiously as Queen Eldora said, 'We can certainly find something special for you and your father to do together, Thomas, but the decision about whether you actually do it will be yours and his. Do you understand that?'

Thomas nodded that he did. 'Oh, and I don't really even *like* fishing,' he added. 'So if you could make it something else, that would be great.'

Queen Eldora promised that she would try and find something special that Thomas and his father would *both* enjoy. 'Now, Lucy,' she said, 'have *you* decided yet what *your* wish is to be?'

'Can I wish for Grandpa's hip to get better?' Lucy asked.

'Oh no, Lucy,' Grandpa said immediately. 'I'm going into hospital for a hip replacement next month. I'd prefer to have the doctors sort that out for me, thanks just the same. No offence to you fairies, of course,' he added hastily.

'No offence taken,' Queen Eldora said, looking amused. 'You will have to think of another wish, Lucy.'

Lucy looked around the table, seeing that a lot of the fairies were getting fidgety now. She hoped they weren't going to be cross with her for making the meeting drag on even longer, but she couldn't help it. 'I think I still need a bit more time to think of something else,' she said apologetically.

Thomas let out an impatient sigh and so did some of the less polite fairies.

'In that case I suggest that we finish this meeting now, and Lucy can come and tell me her wish later on,' Queen Eldora said. 'Izzy and Grandpa, please go with Goldie and Bonnie to the Wing Rooms. Everyone else, please make your way immediately to our fairy party!'

All the fairies started to chatter excitedly as the fairy queen waved her toothbrush over the proceedings and declared the meeting officially ended.

As they flew outside, Lucy and Thomas began to ask Precious questions about the party.

'It will certainly be the best party you've ever been to,' Precious told them, 'as long as you don't expect ordinary food.'

'Why? What sort of food are we having?' Thomas asked.

'Oh ... toothpaste sandwiches, toothpaste biscuits, toothpaste cakes and maybe even toothpaste ice cream if we're lucky,' Precious replied.

'Yuck!' Thomas pulled a disgusted face.

'Well, we *are* tooth fairies,' Precious said, grinning. 'Come on.' She led them away from the main crowd of fairies, who were all heading in the opposite direction. 'I know a short cut to the party. Follow me!'

14

Precious took them along a narrow path that wound round the backs of some tooth-shaped houses and then along a second path that seemed to be taking them back in the direction they'd come from. Finally they stopped at the gates of what seemed to be a park.

'It's very dark here,' Lucy said as Precious led them inside. 'You're not playing some sort of trick on us, are you?'

'A trick?' Precious said, sounding offended. 'As if I would!'

And as she spoke, the area was suddenly lit up by hundreds of fairy lights all coming on at once. '*SURPRISE!*' lots of fairy voices all shouted together, and the children saw that they were in the middle of a huge outdoor party filled with excited tooth fairies in shiny, white party dresses and glowing white wings.

'I took you the long way round so there was time for everyone else to get here first,' Precious said, as some fairy dance-music started up. 'And don't worry, tooth fairies don't really eat toothpaste! We just brush our teeth with it like everybody else!' She led them over to a nearby table, where all the party food was laid out.

'Wow!' Lucy gasped.

There were pink and purple sandwiches, fairy cakes with white icing that glowed in the dark,  rainbow-coloured sausages, gold and silver biscuits and many other amazing things that the children had never seen before.

'All the sweet stuff is made with a magic sugar that's very good for your teeth,' Precious told them, as she picked up a sparkly gold plate and began to load it with food.

'Look, Lucy, here are Izzy and Grandpa,' Thomas said, and Lucy looked up to see her sister and grandfather flying towards

them with Goldie and Bonnie on either side. Izzy was beaming as she showed off her shimmery pink wings, which exactly matched her dress, and Grandpa was smiling too as he flapped his red-and-green-striped wings, which exactly matched his pyjamas.

'This is the first party I've been to in a long time where I haven't had to worry about putting too much weight on my hip,'

Grandpa said, holding out his hand to Izzy and dancing with her in mid-air.

While Thomas went off to talk to some of the boy fairies – or *winged boys* as they preferred to call themselves – Lucy stayed to chat with Precious. 'Did you get into trouble when you got home?' she asked her. 'For stealing all those teeth, I mean.'

'Queen Eldora had a very stern talk with me, yes,' Precious told her. 'She said she was pleased I'd been able to come home but she also said I'd have to work really hard at being good from now on or the same thing might happen to me again. To tell you the truth, I'm a bit scared to *leave* Fairyland now in case it does!'

Lucy frowned as she heard this and, since Bonnie was flying past at that moment, Lucy quickly stopped her and asked to be taken to see the fairy queen.

Queen Eldora was sitting on a gold picnic rug, taking sips from a tall glass of pink bubbly liquid. She motioned for Lucy to sit down beside her and said, 'I presume you've come to tell me that you have decided on your fairy wish?'

Lucy nodded and took a deep breath. She might as well just say it – even though she was a little scared to, now that she was face to face with the fairy queen. 'I'd like you to get rid of the Goodness curtain, please,' she said in a rush.

'I beg your pardon?' Queen Eldora was looking at Lucy as if she had just said that she wanted fairies to get rid of their wings.

'It just doesn't seem like a very *fairy* . . . I mean a very *fair* thing,' Lucy spluttered. 'And it doesn't work as a punishment either. I mean, look at Precious. She got

even naughtier after she was banished from Fairyland – that's why she started stealing all the teeth.'

'Lucy, the Goodness curtain was invented for a reason,' Queen Eldora told her firmly. 'It was invented to stop any Badness entering Fairyland. It is there for our protection.' Queen Eldora was looking at her as if she could hardly believe that a little human girl was questioning one of the most established features of Tooth-fairy Land.

'But couldn't you just ... I don't know ... *change* it so that no tooth fairy ever gets stuck on the other side of it again?' Lucy asked. 'Couldn't you at least have a special meeting to *discuss* changing it or something?'

'A special meeting?' Queen Eldora looked surprised. 'We would need to have *several* meetings to discuss such an important subject, Lucy!'

'That's my wish then,' Lucy put in swiftly. 'That you have as many meetings as you need to at least *discuss* changing the Goodness curtain. Maybe you could all vote on it at the end or something.'

Queen Eldora looked thoughtful. 'Very well then,' she finally agreed. 'Your wish – strange though it is – will be granted.'

As Lucy thanked her and lost no time in getting up to leave, the fairy queen added, 'But because you have not asked for anything for yourself, Lucy, I am going to award you an extra fairy gift.'

'What is it?' Lucy asked.

'Tomorrow, when you wake up, you will find your very own magic toothbrush under your pillow,' the fairy

queen told her. 'Whenever you brush your teeth with it, you will find yourself believing in fairies.'

'But I *already* believe in fairies!'

'*Now* you do, yes,' Queen Eldora said, 'but this toothbrush will be yours to keep forever.'

'But I'm never going to need it!' Lucy protested. 'I'm *never* going to stop believing in fairies.'

'All children say that, Lucy, but one day you will be a grown-up and then you may have more use for this magic toothbrush than you think.'

Lucy frowned because she still wasn't convinced that she was going to get any use at all out of her fairy gift. Unless . . .

'Is it all right to lend it to other people?' She asked. 'People who *don't* believe in fairies – like my mum and dad, for instance?'

'As long as you don't lose it, you may lend it to whoever you wish,' Queen Eldora said. 'Though lending your toothbrush to others doesn't sound very hygienic to me.'

'Don't worry. I'll wash it really well in between times,' Lucy promised. And she began to feel quite excited as she saw how she could put her fairy toothbrush to good use after all. Grandpa had told her that it was only children and old folk who believed in fairies, but maybe he was wrong. Maybe Lucy's mum and dad *could* believe in fairies too – if only they had a magic toothbrush to help them.